Tales from Winderlawk

THE HEIR OF KEMBARIUS

SARAH STEHLIK

For Noah, Sam & Ben,
my loyal tribesmen

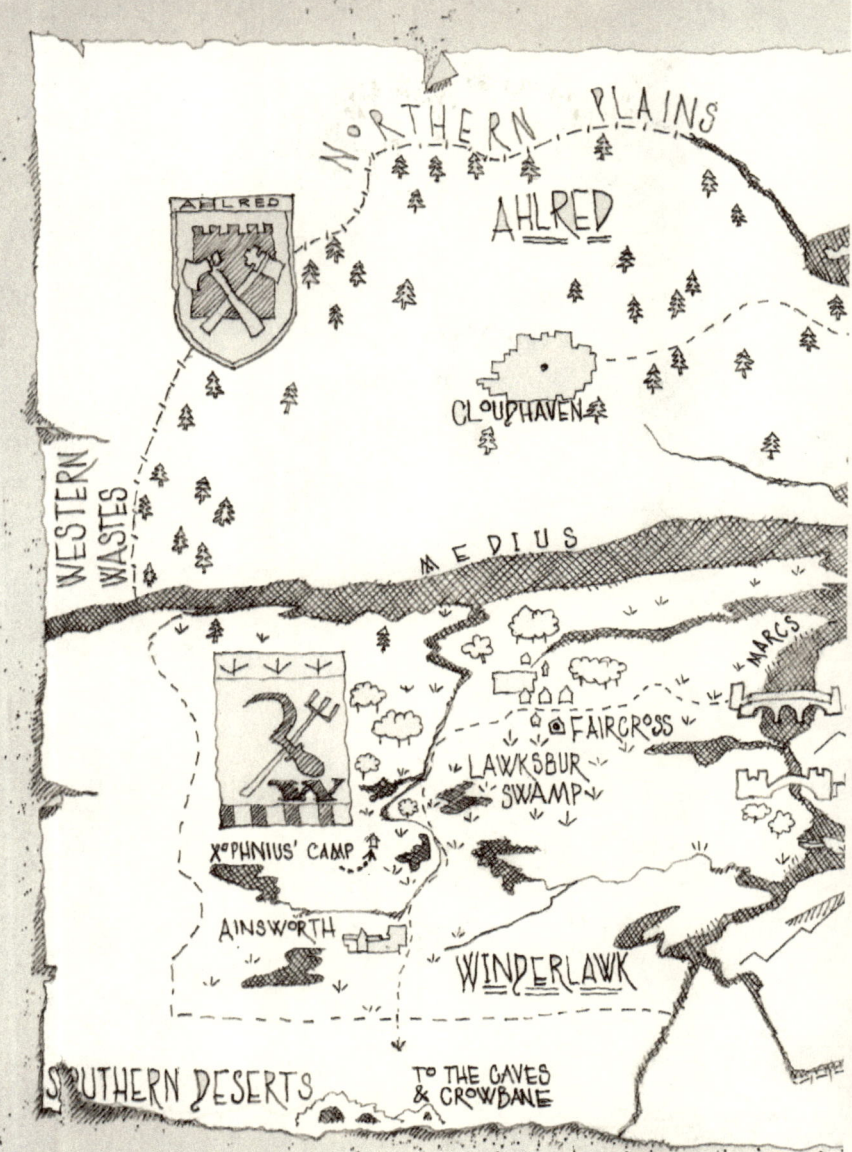

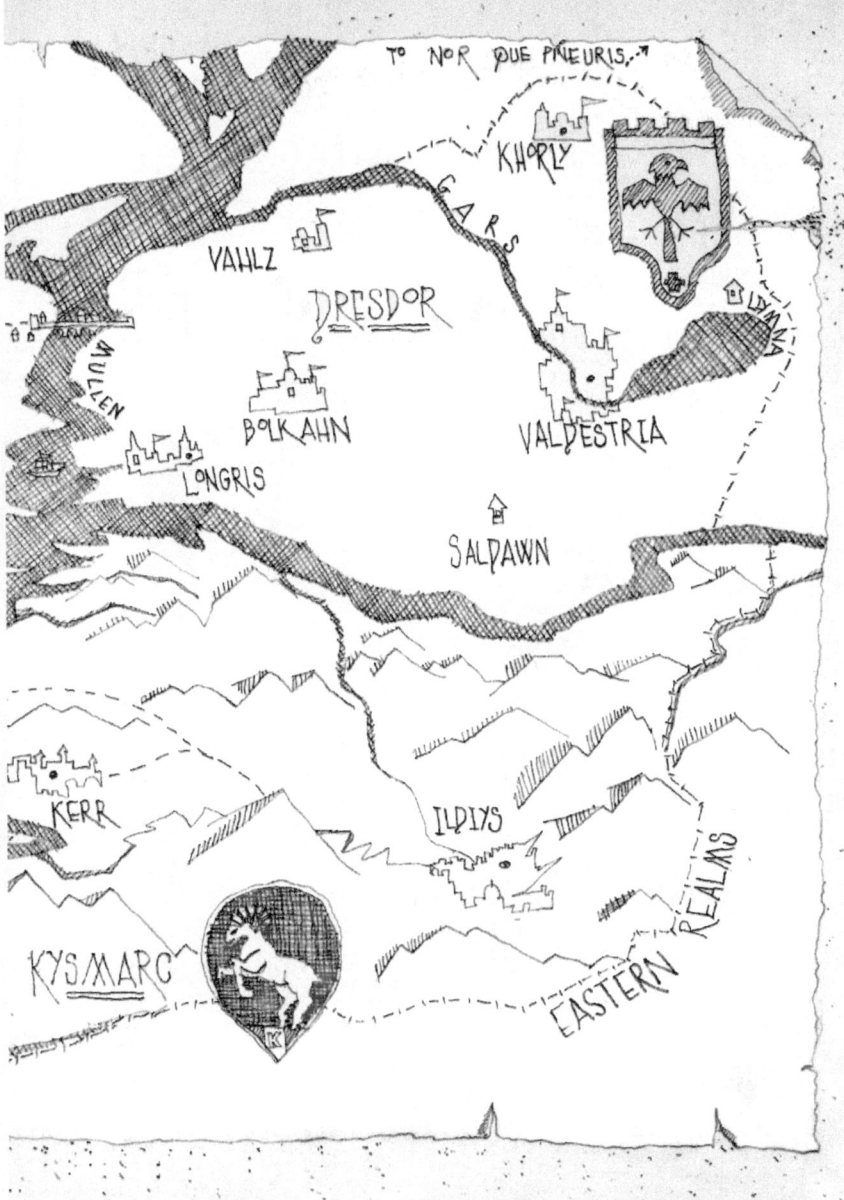

CONTENTS

PROLOGUE i

1 A HISTORY LESSON, OF ALL THINGS 1

2 OUT OF EVERY DARK THING 12

3 A SUMMONS 23

4 SECRETS IN THE NORTH 36

5 A TENTATIVE ALLIANCE 42

6 AN UNIMAGINED FORCE 53

7 HEAVY THINGS 62

8 THE RESISTANCE 72

9 A BITTER WIND BLOWS 81

10 TO THE CAVES 92

11 A BROTHERHOOD BOUGHT 103

12 A WORLD COMES TOGETHER;

A WORLD FALLS APART 114

13 WAR RESOLUTION 126

14 THE RISE OF A KING 136

15 BATTLE PLANS 145

16 TRAITORS OLD AND NEW 154

17 THINGS UNEXPECTED   164

18 UNIONS   175

19 AHMAHNRIC MOVES   185

20 EXCHANGE AT A HIGH PRICE   191

21 BATTLE FOR THE FOUR CORNERS   202

22 THAT I SHARE FOR YOUR HOPE   210

PROLOGUE

"Is this a true story?" some will ask. Well, if you cannot find truth in this story then I will not have told it very well. "But the Four Corners," you will say, "is it a real place and could we ever get there?" Not all real places may be found on all maps, friend, and who am I to tell you where you might go? As for the events of the story itself, where do I begin? I suppose you will want to know how the heir was found. And surely you will want to know if he overcame such treachery as was laid against him, and if, in the end, he was able to restore peace to the tribes who have dwelled throughout the Four Corners of the Earth since the beginning. You might well be wondering how the tribes fared when Ahmahnric and the Eastern Barbarians bore down on them and the great battle ensued. If you have read the Writings of the Elders, you likely have a sinking feeling about that. Or could it be that you have never read the Elders? It is true enough that few in this day have. But since history has a way of repeating itself, perhaps it is worth recalling these words penned by the Elders to the tribes long ago. Though the letter itself is centuries old at the time our story begins, some things do not change so very much over time:

From the Council of the Elders
Written to those in governance of the four tribes
    of Dresdor, Kysmarc, Ahlred, & Winderlawk
On this third summer moon in the first year
    of the 68th Regent of Dresdor:

Pax, brothers. We write to you from Cloudhaven, having met long to discuss the alarming turn of events as was seen at the uprising in Valdestria last fortnight and having been resolved to determine what actions may be taken to turn the tide from animosity to peace again within the Four Corners. We are, in a word, distressed. That you know full well the charge given us ages ago by the great Elethas in the year Kembarius died, we are certain. That we presented to you, this very moon's rising, the rightful heir to Kembarius's throne can hardly be disputed. That you took up arms against this body of Elders and against one another to refuse his rule will be reckoned for when you stand before Elethas at the last, make no mistake about that. Of the heir's whereabouts now, we cannot be sure; but this much do we know and thus do we make our plea to you: if you do not alter your ways, your rebellious disunity will prove your undoing. You look on one another with the eye of an enemy, while an Enemy wholly unmatched waits beyond your walls. How long has it been since Ahmahnric last struck within your borders? Has it been even a handful of years? How quickly you forget, young ones! Submission to a king you desire not, and yet Elethas has ordained that it is the rightful King who will secure your lands and vanquish the shadow of Ahmahnric forever. We implore you, as those who have watched over you from the beginning: Stand together. And if together you are no longer tribes only but a kingdom. And if a kingdom come, then so does a King...

1

A HISTORY LESSON, OF ALL THINGS

"Some say the tribes began as one... back in the age of the ancients. Some say they'll be one again someday. What do you think of that?"

A group of young, plainly dressed boys and girls sat round the feet of their teacher. She was a brown-eyed, fair-skinned girl of eighteen, and Nora Wrenvale was her name. Her students sat silently—even cautiously—for such questions were not the material of common school discussions in the quiet town of Ainsworth, nor in any other town in Winderlawk for that matter.

It was not, in fact, a very popular practice for the Winn (that is, the people of the Winderlawk tribe) to send their children to school at all, proper education not being terribly prized by such folk. For the Winn were, generally speaking, a people who lived simply off the land; and, as such, were content not to concern themselves with the seemingly pointless business of educating their children about irrelevant subjects such as grammar and poetry, mathematics or politics.

It had been discovered in recent times, however, that formal schooling had become a widely embraced practice by the tribe of Dresdor (which only made sense, given the Dresden affinity for enterprise and industry and all things related to human potential and achievement). And the learning of this created a bit of a stir in Winderlawk. For though most of the Winn preferred to carry on as if they were the only tribe in all the Four Corners of the Earth, there were a considerable number who were dismayed with a nagging anxiety that the children of Dresdor were perhaps being given an advantage that Winn children were not—and that it could possibly prove disastrous at some point in the future.

Thus, after much wearying discussion and back-and-forth consideration, it had been decided that Winderlawk should also open a limited number of schools. These were to give children a good introduction to the pillars of Winn life (namely agriculture and the raising of livestock) and were not to burden the children with ridiculous subjects (such as the arts or writing and composition)

"Can you imagine?" Nora asked the students, "Winderlawk and Ahlred, Kysmarc and Dresdor... all one tribe?"

"My father says those is the biggest lies he ever heard," spoke up one boy, bold, with a defiant chin and blond hair shooting in every direction. "He says Winderlawk's got nothing to do with anybody else."

Nora nodded her head slowly and reassuringly, "I didn't promise it was true, did I, Ribley? I only said *some believe*. The oldest Writings of the Elders tell of a king who ruled the Four Corners of the Earth, from Winderlawk to Ahlred, from Kysmarc to Dresdor. He was a good king, named Kembarius the True. Have any of you heard of him?"

Around the circle, eyes stared back blankly and heads shook curiously. On any given day, there were twelve to twenty students who came to the crude, one-room structure designated "school" for that region. On this day, which happened to be in late spring when sheep were expected to be lambing, attendance was predictably weak.

"Ah," Nora said knowingly, "it is ancient history and

not so well known anymore. Kembarius ruled over all the Four Corners of the Earth for many years in an age of peace. He appointed a council of six Elders to advise him in matters of state and chose four wise men, one to govern over each of the four provinces of his kingdom. For a full generation, people enjoyed plenty from the land and freedom from war. But over time, trouble began to grow for Kembarius in his kingdom. Ahmahnric, who had been High Elder of the six, grew restless, hungry for power, and weary of serving another. He decided he would overthrow Kembarius and make himself king instead, so he went about secretly gathering men to his side. But the other five Elders discovered his plan and warned Kembarius, so that when Ahmahnric and his men launched their attack, the king was well prepared and defeated them with speed and force. Ahmahnric was banished to the Outer Regions of the Earth, and it seemed a great victory. But..." Nora paused and began to shake her head.

"What?!" shouted out the young boy Ribley with the wild blond hair and defiant chin. "But what?!"

"The following year, when everyone was gathered to celebrate the anniversary of the traitor Ahmahnric's defeat at the hands of Kembarius the True... that very night, a cry was heard from the royal house. The king's daughter was discovered missing. It was widely believed that Ahmahnric had sent his men to kidnap the young Tsalina—the king's only child—in bitter revenge."

The children all looked on with fear-filled faces. Outside the small school, the sky was growing overcast and the wind was beginning to skip leaves and bits of grass across the gentle hills of Ainsworth. For a moment Nora thoughtfully observed the sky through one of the few square windows. "Hmmm," she murmured uneasily.

"Miss Wrenvale, did King Kembarius get her back?"

asked the smallest of the girls, concern in her thin voice.

"No, Shimrose. He did not," Nora said with a grave sigh. "Kembarius's warriors searched the Four Corners in vain, and the king himself journeyed many times and long into the Outer Regions…" she hesitated, marking anxious expressions on the young faces, "but maybe we will continue another day."

Wild cries of dismay rose up from among the children, as they all begged and whined and pleaded to know what happened to the girl Tsalina and her father who could surely not rest until he found her.

Without warning, a wooden shutter broke loose in a gust of wind and slammed against the wall of the school, sending a wave of frightened roars among the children.

"All right, all right, boys and girls," Nora motioned for them to calm themselves as she made her way over to the window and fastened it tightly shut. Sitting back down in her creaky, well-aged chair and placing young Shimrose in her lap, she continued, "Kembarius was beside himself with grief and was preparing for yet another long and dangerous journey to the Outer Regions in search of Tsalina, when the great spirit Elethas spoke to him."

"My father says there's no such thing at all as the great spirit," interjected Ribley. "He says—"

"But your father is not telling this tale is he now?" said Nora, "and Kembarius, great king of the Four Corners of the Earth, fell knees to the dirt, face to the ground, in awe. Elethas said he had seen the evil worked against this honest man and vowed it would be put to right."

"Did Elethas find the king's daughter?" asked Tredwyl, one of the bigger boys in the back.

"No," answered the teacher, "this is what he told the king: 'Kembarius,' he said, 'your days approach their appointed end, but know that I will be guard of your house. To the Elders, whom you have chosen, I will ordain length of days until your rightful heir is returned to your throne. They shall walk this earth, be it countless ages, until the five have restored to the kingdom what the one has taken.'"

"So the five Elders got to live forever?" asked a girl with curly hair the color of straw.

"Not forever exactly," Nora corrected.

"Only till they finish the task Elethas gave them," offered Tredwyl, "of finding the heir of Kembarius and making him king."

"That's right," nodded Nora, "and yet it is not quite that simple, is it? How many Elders had Kembarius chosen?"

"Six," answered several of the students.

"Indeed. Six. And so there are six who lived ages ago, and who live still until the heir of Kembarius is given the throne and the vow of Elethas is fulfilled."

"But I think Ahmahnric sounds awful!" shuddered Shimrose, "I don't want him to be alive still."

"Aw, good grief Shim, it's not real. It's just stories," said Ribley in a condescending voice.

"*Is* it real, Miss Wrenvale?" asked one of the other girls. Shimrose snuggled her head against her teacher's shoulder, as the children launched all kinds of questions about the tale, until Nora raised a finger to her lips and silenced all the eager voices.

"Listen," she began but noticed Tredwyl's hand raised high in the air. "Yes, Tredwyl?"

The boy of ten years with a serious face, dark blue eyes, and the dirt of a farm boy always smudged up around them answered, "Miss Wrenvale, how did the tribe become four then?"

"Yes, back to the point of this history lesson.

Kembarius died not very long after Elethas had spoken to him. And the kingdom wept with sorrow. Without an heir who would become king now? The people were quite in despair until finally the Elders announced that the kingdom should be entrusted to the governors of the four provinces until the rightful ruler should be crowned."

"And those provinces became the four tribes?" asked Tredwyl.

"Certainly," said Nora.

The boy shook his head curiously, "But if they were one people, why do they despise each other so much now?"

Nora sighed, set Shimrose back down at her feet, and replied, "The answer to that question is very long and quite complicated—"

"And not at all what you expect to hear at a school in Winderlawk," came a voice from the doorway. A young man, tall and strong, stood leaning against the open door with a good-natured smile on his face. He was dressed much like every other man of Winderlawk who spends his days living off the earth- with the loose sleeves of his handspun shirt pushed up to the elbows and his dark cotton trousers rolled up about his calves. His bare feet defied shoes as much as his brown windblown hair defied order at the moment.

"Fen!" shouted several of the children as Nora nodded to their visitor, a resolute look about her eyes.

"Hello, Fen," she said, trying to mask her delight with a cool confidence and very nearly succeeding. "What a surprising disruption to our history lesson. How can I help you?"

"History?!" responded Fen, walking over to the group and looking with a questioning smile at the students. "Has the most excellent Miss Wrenvale not been teaching you your planting rhythms, your water systems?"

Several of the children were nodding eagerly and promising that she had. Some were even starting to recite the beginner's chart for the Winderlawk Planting Cycle, but Nora stood imperiously, and quieted the children, fixing a pleasant but challenging stare at the young man who stood grinning before her. "Surely you did not come into this school to challenge my teaching methods."

Fen bowed his head deeply in surrender. "Miss Wrenvale, freely I confess you are quite a more capable teacher than I would ever make, and for the disruption I beg your pardon. Certainly your students know my respect for you runs as far as the Four Corners of the Earth and back."

The girls in the circle giggled quietly, and Nora rolled her eyes a bit with a smile and a shake of her long, dark hair.

"I did not come to disrupt *history* (of all things to hear in school)," Fen continued, "I came to walk you home. A storm is swelling… from the south."

Some of the young children squealed, and a few started to their feet anxiously.

"Settle down, little Winn, settle down," Nora quieted them. "I think Fen is right that we should be going. The wind has been picking up all afternoon, but you should have plenty of time to get to your farms if you don't stop to play along the way."

A mad rush of children hurried for the door, as she shouted out, "And when you come tomorrow make sure to bring your seedlings! We'll be working in the garden!"

The room was empty of children in a moment, except Tredwyl, who stood looking long at Miss Wrenvale. She worked about the room briefly, tidying up the children's worktables and putting away her things; and then looking up, she noticed him. "Yes?"

Tredwyl looked down at the ground uncomfortably for a moment, and then found his words, "My parents say that Winderlawk has no need to be dealing with the other tribes. They say no Winn has any business believing in the Elders. That's the way of the Ahlrik, they say. Maybe even the Kysmen, but not the Winn."

Fen looked sharply at Nora, who hesitated a bit at her pupil's plain words and finally nodded her head gently. "That is the feeling of most, Tredwyl. Your parents are quite in the majority of Winderlawk."

"You believe it's all true though, don't you Miss Wrenvale?" Tredwyl's blue eyes searched his young teacher's face. But Fen walked briskly over to Nora, holding out her cloak and turning to Tredwyl, "You'll be needing to get home now. If the storm brings the mastids you'll not want to be caught this side of the ferry."

It was true enough. Storms from the south often meant trouble for the people of Winderlawk who lived south of the Lawksbur Swamp. It was not always, yet neither was it uncommon, that the south winds would stir swarms of mastids, furious bat-like hunters (though quite larger than bats), into a frenzy across the lower lands of Winderlawk. And the mention of them snapped the young boy with questions into the business of leaving quickly.

"Don't forget your seedlings!" Nora called out after him and took her cloak from Fen. She wrapped the thick gray wool around her square shoulders and pulled her hair out from under it. The sounds of the howling wind outside grew louder, and she peeked out the doorway before one last trip to her desk for a small canvas satchel that she tucked well under her cloak and hung over her shoulder.

"Nora Wrenvale..." began Fen in a big brotherishly reprimanding sort of way.

"You're right about the storm. It's gotten a bit worse than I'd thought it would. I'm glad you came," she answered quickly as she headed for the door, patting him on the shoulder as she passed by.

He followed immediately behind her, still firm in his tone, "You know you oughtn't be telling the kids those stories."

The two emerged onto a dirt road, with the wind blowing in force all around them. Tredwyl was speeding north very nearly out of sight already. (Winderlawk children are commonly considered unnaturally fleet of foot.) The sky had quickly grown well darker than its true hour, and great clouds could be seen churning just off in the south.

"Swampish luck and muck, it got bad so fast," Nora said disdainfully.

"You're avoiding my point," said Fen, putting a hand at her back and guiding them briskly along the dirt road that cut northward across a mass of low, grassy hills.

Nora lifted her eyes to the wooded horizon a little less than a mile or so off that marked the edge of the Lawksbur Swamp, where the ferry worked to carry passengers between the northern and southern lands of Winderlawk.

"I'm avoiding nothing," she answered plainly.

"Is that right?" Fen responded with an incredulous tone.

She gripped her cloak around herself as they hurried on. "I am a teacher. I teach. It's not so criminal as you make it sound, Fen."

"Don't turn things around like that, Nora. Teaching school is one thing. Telling stories that get people all worked up is another. You know that little Ribley Hollowsman is likely to go straight to his father and tell him exactly—"

"Tell him exactly what?!" Nora stopped and turned with a defiant spark in her eyes. "Do you think I'm ashamed of myself? That I'm telling the children *secrets*? Let them tell their parents all of it. Let them read the Writings of the Elders for themselves—"

"Fire and thunder, Nora! What is it that gets into you?" Fen's exasperated voice rose above the wind's eerie howls. "Wars have started over the Writings of the Elders!"

"Wars have started over a lot of things. And you needn't worry... I'm not quite breeding an army of children yet. Ugh!" Nora stamped off a few paces and then turned back, looking the solid young man straight in the eyes.

It was a certain reality of their long friendship that she was prone to be stubborn and that he was prone to provoke it and that arguing seldom proved advantageous to either of the two. For the moment they stood locked still, squarely facing the other while the wind whipped through her hair and round her cape and the first drops of an angry rain began to pelt.

Fen finally shook his finger at Nora and spoke slowly at first, "Nora Wrenvale, I've known you since you were too little to ride a goat. And I still don't understand you."

Nora squinted a look of disapproval. "And I've known you just as long and I don't believe you think they're just *stories*. Not for a minute. You know they're true—"

Fen started to interrupt, but her fiery voice only grew more determined, "YOU KNOW THEY'RE TRUE. You know it, and I know you know it. What I don't know is why you *fear* it so much."

Those last words came out with a bit more bite than Nora had intended, and she regretted them almost immediately, as is so often the case for those who draw speech from the well of quick passion. But in the next moment, she had all but forgotten her regret; for they both realized they had made a terrible mistake. They knew it the moment the first mastid came into sight.

2

OUT OF EVERY DARK THING...

If you have never been caught in a Winderlawk southern storm with an onslaught of raging mastids flying in, you may well find it difficult to appreciate the seriousness of the situation in which Fen and Nora now found themselves.

For a moment, Nora stood frozen, watching with horror as the winged creatures came closing in. Fen looked urgently in every direction for the most promising refuge—a boulder, a tree, anything which might shield them at least from some point; but there was nothing on the grassy open hills within two hundred horse lengths. And they were less than half-way to the protection that would have been afforded them by the swamp.

"We can't make that distance!" Nora shouted above the storm.

Fen rapidly blinked the rain drops out of his eyes and looked frantically from Nora to the mastids, that were now moments away from them. "I've cost us something now," he muttered. In a leap, he was standing between her and the coming hunters, and he pulled swiftly at the tie of her cloak.

"Get down!" he shouted. "Cover your head!" She was on the ground before she knew it, hidden beneath a mantle of woolen gray. It was most definitely not the first time she had experienced a mastid attack, and she hated the beasts with all her might. Once, it had been her and her mother. They had been visiting a family in Ainsworth who was celebrating a new baby when one of the fierce southern storms had struck without warning. Fortunately, they had been on horseback then. Well is it known that if anything has the power to put fear in the horses of Winderlawk, it is the mastids from the Southern Caves. Nora and her mother had all but flown to the ferry that day, the horses rushing like the wind while the hearts of mother and child pounded like drums.

Why the mastids would not venture into the swamp was largely a disputed mystery to the Winn. Some said it was the swamp air, that it was troublesome in some way for them. Others said the swamp must be home to some hidden creature (or creatures), known to the mastids and wholly feared by them. Whatever the reason, the Lawksbur Swamp remained the bounds of safety, a line of demarcation which separated the more prosperous Winn of the northern lands from their less fortunate tribesmen of the south- Winn who had to deal with unfortunate realities like unpredictable mastids and swamp floods in the early spring.

At the sound of Fen's first cry of pain, Nora shouted with a muffled wildness, "Fen! Are you all right?!"

He was certainly not all right. He was, in fact, even less all right than he perceived—and he did not think himself very well off to begin with. Fen had fought off mastids since his youngest days in the fields. He couldn't have been more than seven years old the first time he stood in front of a herd of wild-eyed sheep, blundering and bleating in chaotic terror, and raised his small knife to the sky with a war shout to defy an oncoming swarm.

But things had been changing over the years. The mastids were far greater in number when they came these days and, it seemed, more aggressive. Though it had been told when Fen was a boy that mastid fang and talon could pull apart a goat, it was rare that anyone had actually seen it or even seen evidence of it. These days such brutality happened with unnerving regularity.

"Fen!?" Nora could almost feel the beat of leathery wings just above her and could hear the strain of Fen's efforts to fight off the creatures. Their throaty, piercing shrieks made her skin crawl.

Most problematic for Fen at the moment, was that he had no weapon. No knife, no spear, no sword. Not even a staff. He found himself in the uncommon predicament of having absolutely nothing with which to make a reasonable defense, and he rebuked himself sternly for having walked off to the school empty-handed.

Nora heard a severe cry followed by a heavy thud, which she feared was his body collapsing on the ground near her; and she screamed in spite of the fact that she had promised herself she would master the panic that was building in her.

"They will be on me in seconds," her thoughts raced. And what could she possibly do? Lie there and let Fen be torn to shreds? Get up and be torn to shreds herself? The dirty smell of the mastids and their merciless noise shook her brain, and she called desperately for him again. There was no answer.

It was quite better that Nora could not see the struggle that had been taking place all around her. For as quickly as Fen had beaten one off, another was on him. His left arm which was almost constantly shielding his face had caught the razor sharp talons numerous times, so that the burning of the wounds began to be almost unbearable.

He was lying on the ground now, a few feet away from Nora. In his mind he was telling himself to stand up and fight, but at each moment a fresh rip of a talon took his breath away. And it was the fangs that sank deep into

14

the base of his neck that made everything grow black and still and silent.

Suddenly, Nora heard an explosive blast followed by the shout of a man's deep voice. There was the frenzied shrieking and beating of wings, as the mastids retreated in a torrent; and in the next breath everything was eerily quiet. Even the rain had abruptly ceased. Nora could hear nothing besides her own shaky breaths; and though she commanded her hand to pull back the cloak so that she might see Fen and know what was happening, her arm refused, weighted helplessly to the ground.

It seemed she passed hours—days—in that cold wet heap on the ground. When at last her trembling hands lifted her cover and she pulled herself up, what Nora saw made her gasp aloud. And possibly she started to cry, though she does not at all recall doing so.

A blood-stained body lie quite still a few feet away. Over it, knelt a man whom Nora had never seen before. He wore a long black tunic, belted at the waist, that covered the tops of something like boots made of worn leather. Just reaching his wide shoulders was his silver hair, though he did not appear to have the age to warrant it. He rather looked neither old nor young and, at the moment, neither friendly nor fierce. A massive gray mare stood behind him, switching her black tail and snorting at the air as if displeased to still smell remnants of the mastids.

"You'll come too of course," the man said, apparently to Nora though he did not look at her, for he continued to examine Fen's wounds with a studied focus.

Nora tried to speak. She opened her mouth but found no words would come. Fen's body lie so miserably motionless on the ground. She saw the red. She saw the torn gray fabric of his shirt hanging in shreds. She saw the gashes. She looked anxiously at the man who looked carefully down at her friend, and finally she managed a whispered, "Is he alive?"

The stranger nodded silently and in a moment added, "Though I have not brought what he needs. Fortunately, we will find it at my camp. You'll have to walk as we'll need the horse for your friend."

Nora agreed with a quivering nod and fumbled her way to her feet. She watched as the man lifted Fen with remarkable strength onto his horse and then turned to her. "Shall we?"

It was then that Nora more fully noticed the ghastly scene around her, for as she began to step towards the stranger, she found her footing difficult. And looking down to steady her stance, she saw the bodies of dead mastids lying heaped in every direction. There could have been a hundred of them, and she immediately closed her eyes and took a deep breath to compose herself.

The man reached his hand out for her with a calming manner, "If we're going to help your friend, we mustn't stand here admiring his exceptional giftedness for boxing mastids."

In a few small steps, Nora had crossed over to the man and his horse and taken his hand. Her eyes took in Fen's condition with worry. The man whispered something in the horse's ear, to which the horse immediately responded by wheeling around and heading steadily in a northwesterly direction. Meanwhile, the mysterious friend walked with a purposeful stride, Nora beside him, eyes fixed directly ahead.

"How did you scare them away?" Nora asked at length.

"By whatever means I could, child," came his brief answer.

"Where do you live? Are you from Winderlawk?" she questioned further.

"I am not precisely from Winderlawk, and my camp you shall see for yourself in short time."

They walked in a heavy quiet for a bit, until Nora felt up to pressing her growing curiosity further. "You say he needs something at your camp. What does he need?"

The clouds were clearing out nearly as quickly as they had rolled in, and blue sky was already beginning to peek through with the promise of sun. The man paused and looked upwards thoughtfully, "Out of every dark thing, hides a secret good that may yet be born." He turned to Nora with a smile that was somehow quite reassuring even though he offered nothing she found particularly helpful in response to her question; and he continued on without another word. The words stuck in Nora's head; she had heard them before. Or at least she thought they sounded familiar. She walked on without speaking, deep in thought, for the entire rest of the journey (which proved to be well longer than she had anticipated).

The man's camp lay on the edges of the swamp itself but some distance west of the ferry, in a spot that made one feel it was quite remote and wild. The man set to work at once, carrying Fen into his cozy dwelling that actually appeared much larger when you were on the inside of it than you would have expected from the outside of it.

Nora did not notice, until entering, that there were no windows in the place, making the sense of privacy overwhelming. The man made directly for a small fire which had been left going in the hearth, and in time he had a dull, silver pot with various leaves and roots and a dark thick liquid of some sort all mixed together and simmering over the crackling flames. A heavy blanket he handed to Nora in exchange for her wet gray cloak. She gratefully bundled up inside its warmth and took a seat next to Fen who was laid out on a cushioned bench near the fire.

"There were so many," she said, shaking her head. "I can't imagine if you hadn't come when you did." Nora looked to the man, and he smiled kindly in return. "I don't know your name," she added politely.

He gave her a bright-eyed look and, with a decisive nod, straightened up honorably and answered, "I am Xophnius, young Winn, and I am pleased to be of help to you and your friend today."

At the name "Xophnius" Nora's eyes locked on the man with an intense fascination.

"Xophnius?" she repeated.

"Yes," he replied and stepped over to stir the pot and check its bubbling contents. The glow of the fire was warm and soothing in the dark little cottage.

"*Xophnius?*" she said again.

"Why should you become so fixated?" he asked with perhaps the slightest bit of mirth hidden in his voice.

"It's an uncommon name, sir," Nora replied.

"True enough."

"However, there has been one Xophnius of whom I knew," the girl continued.

"Is that so?"

She nodded.

"Was he a decent sort of fellow? The kind who might aid young unfortunates from grisly mastid attacks? Or was he of the other sort?" Xophnius raised his eyebrows inquisitively. He carefully removed the pot from the fire and set it on the table. Dipping a large wooden spoon into its contents, he emptied a bit of the concoction onto a white cloth that lay next to the pot. And taking the cloth in one hand, he gently lifted Fen's head with the other and pressed the cloth over the puncture wounds in his neck.

An almost imperceptible grimace flashed across the

face of the wounded, but it was immediately noticed by both friend and doctor. It appeared to encourage the latter. He dipped his spoon back into the pot and began soaking another cloth, nodding positively. "There is nothing like the virtues of swamp mud for dealing with injuries of this nature."

Nora inadvertently turned her nose up at the statement and then found herself distracted by a rather gruesome oddity.

"Xophnius?" she asked nervously, as the man applied another cloth to Fen's left arm.

"Yes?"

"What's happening?" She was watching the wound on the base of Fen's neck as a wretched sort of froth appeared to be leaking from the fang holes.

Xophnius replied, "The remedy is drawing out the poison."

"Poison!?"

"Hmm."

Fen's eyes were beginning to flutter a bit and by the creases taking shape in his face, it was evident that the sensation of pain was starting to bring him around.

Nora was perplexed by Xophnius's reply. "I've never heard mastids to be poisonous. Loathsome, yes. But poisonous…" she shook her head in uncertainty.

A look came over Xophnius that Nora did not quite understand. He walked slowly over to a nearby shelf where a few basic kitchen items were stacked, and began work preparing a late coffee for them all.

"They were not always so," he said eventually.

A weak voice rasped out a broken, "Fire and—," Fen attempted to lift his head but gave up instantaneously, "thunder, someone tell me what happened."

Xophnius took a kettle of steaming water, poured it into crude mugs of brown pottery, and began stirring in mounds of coarse crystals black as pitch. It sent a comforting, rich aroma of coffee wafting throughout the room. "Excellent," he said, clearly pleased and relieved to hear the voice of his patient.

Nora's face too spread into a relieved smile of approval, and she stood to see Fen better—or rather to allow him to see her without straining.

"Mastids, Fen. Heaps of them," Nora began.

Fen reached for his left shoulder and winced. He also realized abruptly that his surroundings were a matter of immediate question. "I remember that now. But I do not remember this place."

Xophnius brought the mugs over to the two and set them on the table near Fen's station. "Surely not," he remarked, "but take care a moment." And lifting Fen's body with every gentleness, Xophnius propped him up with a few extra cushions—soft, thick billows of rich wool onto which Fen rested with ease and gratitude.

"Sir, I feel that I am certain to owe you steeply," Fen offered, as Xophnius managed to provide him a few careful sips of the hot brew.

Nora was quick to speak, covering every detail in overwhelming fashion, which was so often her way. Fen tried to listen intently, while Xophnius inspected the puncture again and continued working over him. Truthfully, Fen was largely wishing that his caregiver might suggest to Nora that the patient needed rest and that she might pick up the tale of their events at a later time when his vision was not so blurry and his brain not so beaten by the task of processing what seemed an impossible amount of words.

"But Fen," she rattled on, "you won't imagine how many of them you spent—and without your knife!" A damp strand of Fen's dark hair hung down over his right eye, and she brushed it away apologetically, continuing with a quieter tone, "Please do not even mention that I accused you of fear the moment before you battled and I ducked. Rot on me, Fen. We'll get you home soon, and Grable will be so proud. He won't believe how many mastids you wrung."

At her words, Fen inescapably slipped back into a hard sleep, but they clearly sparked an interest in Xophnius.

"Would you mean Grable Lawk?" he asked Nora with a gravity that she seemed to miss.

"Yes. Do you know him?" Nora replied.

"I do not precisely know him," Xophnius answered carefully. "Does the boy stay with him?"

Nora sipped her coffee and answered with a simple, "Yes."

"But he is not..." Xophnius paused as if thinking to himself and studying Fen's face, "that is to say, the boy is not... he is not Grable's son?"

"No," Nora said. "Fen never knew his parents. Grable took him in when he was a baby and has been so much like a father to him."

Xophnius looked hard at the young man, doubtful and inquisitive murmurs playing quietly across his lips. Finally, he seemed to grumpily dismiss it all, turned to Nora and gave a long sigh. "No doubt you are tired and would like to go home, dear. Your friend, however, most certainly need stay and rest. Perhaps you would be willing to let me send you home on my horse while I stay to see to his condition."

"I would be grateful for it, sir," said Nora, realizing for the first time since the whole horrific scene on the road and amidst her concern for Fen, how sincerely tired and weak she did feel.

She took another sip from the warm cup in her hands and closed her eyes for a moment. Images of the last few hours played rapidly without permission through her mind, and at the blur of a silver-haired figure bowing in introduction before her she shook herself back to the present. Opening her eyes, she peered up at him. "Just before I go, I have a question," she said.

But Xophnius had walked to the doorway and given a low whistle, the tone of it hung solidly in the heavy swamp air as one's coat might hang on a hook. He smiled a gracious but weary smile to Nora, "Child, there are more questions than can be answered this evening. Let us leave them where they may be picked up tomorrow."

The gray mare was now standing at the door, and Nora raised herself to her feet with a last glance towards Fen. The wound in his neck still bubbled and oozed but the look on his face suggested a restful sleep.

At the doorway she looked up into the face of the kindly gentleman, gratitude brimming in her weary eyes.

"She will take you home if you will tell her the way. And she will bring you back when it is time."

Nora looked questioningly from man to beast. "She will know?"

"Precisely," he answered and helped her mount. He whispered again in the horse's ear and bade the young woman farewell. But she turned at the last moment as the horse began to trot off, "Xophnius, what is her name?"

He smiled broadly and waved goodbye saying, "Gracious, child, I alone know that." And he disappeared back into the soft, warm light of the cottage.

As it happened, there was another figure as well who disappeared from the scene, but this one went not into the shelter of the cottage but into the shadows of the swamp. And he went wholly unnoticed by anyone.

3

A SUMMONS

Before we are able to follow Fen and Xophnius and their encounter with each other (that profoundly altered them both), we must first turn our attention directly east of Winderlawk, to where the tribe of Kysmarc dwells. Headed eastward the gentle hills of Winn country give way to a more mountainous terrain of stunning beauty. Rugged slopes rise sharply from lakes of crystal; valleys blanketed with wildflowers are tucked between steep hillsides of vibrant green.

Kysmarc is a land alive and the Kysmen who dwell there equally spirited. They are not given much to the heavy farming ways of the Winn, with long hours in the fields and carefully planned rhythms of planting and harvesting. Such lively folk as the Kysmen are not to be burdened by the disciplines and drudgery of such routine.

That is not to say that the men and women of Kysmarc do not work at all—or that they do not enjoy the fruit of the land. Indeed, the orchards and vineyards of Kysmarc have well been known throughout the entire Four Corners as matchless. Apples, crisp to the bite and sweet to the taste, grow inexplicably and magnificently year-round. Winding, leafy grapevines seem to flourish by the sheer will of the earth and little else. Pockets of orange and mango groves can be easily found nestled next to one of the many cool, clear rivers that nourish the countryside from border to border.

It was at an early hour of the morning, with the pale

light of first day just creeping across the sky, that a woman exited quietly through an iron gate, ornate in its fashioning, which let her out from a light and airy chateau onto a mountainside path of smooth gray stone. Her long, loose gown of pearly white flowed behind her in the cool breeze of the morning, and a short cape of white fur, pure and soft, hung about her shoulders down to her slender waist.

She stepped gracefully along the gray stonework, proceeding slowly across the winding, terraced cut in the mountain. Bright, clear notes of bird song echoed gently about the landscape as the light spilling over the peak gradually grew warmer with a rosy orange hue.

By the time the woman reached the towering, stone residence towards which she had been making her way, the glow of morning was in full thrust, lighting her pale golden hair with a shimmering brilliance. She did not need knock at the iron gates, for they were swung open for her and waiting when she came within sight, as if the gardener attached to her a sense of royalty or, at the very least, nobility. She nodded slightly to him as she passed through without pause, seeing, at once, the purpose of her early outing.

A table stood low to the grassy lawn, surrounded by thick pillows of raw silk. It lay in the center of a lush garden setting, filled with climbing vines and oversized dark green foliage, neatly trimmed trees and bursts of flowers of all kinds—sprays of white and yellow roses, shoots of sweet peas and snapdragons in vivid indigos and deep crimsons. Ferns cast forth their delicate fronds from the shady beds beneath giant, purple-leafed pear trees (an exotic and delicious variety).

The table itself was covered with a shining white cloth, upon which was set porcelain platters of breads and cheeses and fruits. Wines of various pinks and whites filled an assortment of bottles that stood mingling amidst an exquisite collection of wild orchids brought for the morning spread.

Rising like an arrow from his cushioned seat was a man of generous size and dark complexion. Long dark hair flowed down his back; the color made one think of rich, upturned earth. And he wore a smile as he took the fair, outstretched hand of the woman, giving it the lightest kiss.

"Welcome, Bryn. Join me this fresh morning," his strong voice greeted her. His name was Kholrihk, and they had known each other quite some time, as you will come to understand.

"Thank you," she replied, and they both settled themselves onto their pallets, legs crossed, bodies as effortlessly erect as the orchids.

They spent no small time talking of nothing in particular, giving most of their attention to the sweetness of the strawberries or the impeccable pairing of this cheese and that wine. A fountain of hammered copper bubbled in the corner of the garden, where a vast array of birds gathered to glean their breakfasts from the damp surrounding earth; and the pair of humans watched them contentedly for some time as if there were no other business of the day—or perhaps as if that very occupation *was* the business of the day.

It was not. But it is not the way of the Kysmen to rush into formalities of business without spending sufficient time enjoying one's company with no intrusion of pressing need. As a full hour had now passed, though, and half of the next as well, it was time to begin moving in the direction of specific matters, for which tea is very nearly always requisite in Kysmarc. So as a tray bearing a glimmering silver tea set was additionally brought out by one of the house servants and arranged before the two friends, the woman—Bryn—began to speak of the nature of her errand.

"Xophnius has sent word. A carrier arrived at my window in the mid hours of the night, and I am unsure of the message I should send in response."

Kholrihk held up his cup, taking in the fragrance of the lemongrass steam. "What is his news?" he asked.

"What is ever his news? 'Perhaps he has found something.' 'Perhaps we have missed something.' He summons us to his camp on the Lawksbur immediately for council. One would assume he has likewise already summoned the others."

Bryn watched a robin by the fountain as he pecked swiftly at the smallest of grasshoppers. He was disappointed his first attempt and darted quickly towards his meal's subsequent position only to be beaten again. The scene went on like this, and Bryn observed thoughtfully.

"He is certainly well meaning," Kholrihk said, "he always has been."

"No one can say otherwise," Bryn turned back to face him. "The question one must ask is: toward what end?"

Kholrihk nodded in agreement. "Have you any leanings as to what our word should be?"

Bryn meditated deliberately on the question before speaking. "I am not inclined to pick up on a pin and make for that odious swamp to satisfy another of his impulsive intuitions—however worthy a friend he might be. What is your thought?"

After a moment of reflection Kholrihk answered, "Let him come here. It is a long distance between this place and his. If his feelings are strong enough on the matter he will make the trouble to come, and we will learn something as to the merit of the situation. If he will not come, then his convictions were likely shaky and unworthy of any urgent energy being spent on our part."

His response seemed to suitably satisfy Bryn, and she rose lightly to her feet. "I will send the bird this very morning. He will have his answer before nightfall."

******

The morning that was bright and fair in the mountains of Kysmarc was hazy and damp in the Lawksbur Swamp. And the two men who found themselves taking breakfast together in the secluded cottage dined quite differently as well.

A bowl of plain, thick oat porridge sat before each man as well as a cup of something like cranberries, dried and seasoned with a gingery cinnamon coating. Each had a mug of blackest coffee, and this was the sum total of the meal.

They had talked little the previous night during Fen's brief waking episodes, covering the most basic of personal introductions and the most pressing issues related to Fen's condition. Now with a full night's sleep and well-treated with Xophnius's remedy, Fen was feeling quite almost his usual self and eager to learn more about the mysterious, heroic swamp-dweller.

"Xophnius, how long have you been in Winderlawk?" Fen asked, popping a dried berry into his mouth.

"Oh," he answered, "sometimes it seems forever."

"There is something very different about you though," said Fen, "something very unlike most Winn."

"I suppose that is true," conceded Xophnius. "I have traveled much and long outside Winderlawk. One is always shaped by different places and experiences."

"Have you been throughout all the Four Corners

then?"

"And elsewhere," Xophnius replied, "but you have been brought up here only, yes?"

Wishing that the man was more inclined to share his story but sensing that he was not, Fen simply answered, "Yes. I have always lived in Winderlawk—or I suppose I should say for as long as I can remember."

"You were not born here then?"

"Who knows?" said Fen. "I never knew my parents—who they were or where they were from. I was left as a baby on the steps of a simple farmer in Ainsworth, the best of men whose wife had recently passed on."

The dark eyes of Xophnius were fixed on the honest face of the young man before him, and he listened with absolute attention.

"He's raised me like a son, Grable has." Fen took a drink of his coffee and gingerly stretched his sore arm and shoulder. His own ragged, blood-stained shirt had been replaced by a soft, clean white tunic that Xophnius had given him, which now hung loosely about his bandaged body.

"And his wife? How did she die?" asked Xophnius, pointedly.

A mournful look crept over Fen's face. "Grable doesn't speak of her. It's very difficult for him I think, even still. I believe she was ill for some time and taken somewhere to be treated, but…" his voice trailed off.

"Her name was Westerlyn, was it not?" asked Xophnius.

Fen's eyes snapped from sorrow to surprise in an instant, "You knew her?"

"Not so very much, no. I knew of her. Somewhat," Xophnius replied. "Odd that you should have been left in the care of a widower in the unlikely town of Ainsworth."

He was not completely sure why, but Fen felt uncomfortable with Xophnius's comments and so remarked, "I've a feeling there are oddities on both our sides, sir."

The older man smiled with a sparkle in his eyes and answered, "That is more than a fair assumption, friend. Quite." And draining the last of his coffee his voice took a lighter tone, "And the girl who was with you yesterday?"

"Nora and I have been friends since our beginnings."

"A neighbor?"

"Hardly," Fen replied with a bit of a laugh. "Her father could lose most of his fortune and still have more than enough means to live north of the Lawksbur. No, she is a Faircross girl, not an Ainsworth one."

Now that they had finished their breakfast, Xophnius motioned him over to the bench near the fire so that he could look over his wounds.

"How then the unlikely friendship?"

Gathering Fen's left sleeve up to his shoulder, Xophnius gently began pulling back bandages on his arm, occasionally applying a fresh dose of mud paste from the silver pot. A far-off look settled over Fen as he considered Xophnius's question and thought back on his younger years.

"Nora is like her mother," Fen paused, "and perhaps her mother is like you." Xophnius's eyes questioned such a statement. "Not very Winn-like in many ways," Fen explained. "Some have claimed she's not from Winderlawk at all. They say she is Ahlrik, though I don't know. But she's always had a compassion for the southern Winn and their struggles. I suppose she spends as much time south of the Lawksbur as north of it, taking food or medicine, caring for those passing on... She was a help to Grable when I first came, and she continued to come through all my young years. Brought her daughter with her most days. I guess Nora is the only friend I've— aghh!" Fen jerked his body away from Xophnius's touch, shielding his neck protectively with his hand. "What in the Four Corners..." he mumbled sulkily.

"My apologies. But the last of the poison must be drained," came the sincere response from Xophnius.

Fen looked at him doubtfully and then reluctantly lowered his hand. He took a deep breath and then rambled on to take his mind off the unpleasant procedure, "The other children—as you might imagine— had no interest in the likes of an orphan. They were fairly merciless when I was younger, but it never occurred to Nora that I should be any different from any other boy in Winderlawk."

Xophnius quoted softly, "The soul who loves beyond reason and practicality is worth a thousand who excuse themselves from the inconvenience." It was quiet for a moment. Then Xophnius took a step back and looked at Fen intently, "Have you ever read the Writings of the Elders?"

Fen stood awkwardly to his feet and stared back with an unsettled expression. Outside, the morning was progressing with the sun beginning to burn off the misty gray, but all of that was shut out of the wooden cocoon that held two men studying each other carefully.

"Sir, I'm not sure of your story. And I've not read the Writings of the Elders—I'll not wish that any different. Winderlawk is not the place for such things, a truth—if you'll permit me to say—which all your travels may have erased from your recollection."

They stood looking at each other what seemed like a very long time but which was actually a rather short time, with an exasperation building in Xophnius. It was evident to Fen, and he attempted to ease the tense situation, "I hope you do not take me rude; I am most grateful for the help you given me. You have likely been the difference in my life and in its end... but let's not speak of things that are needlessly troublesome."

"Needlessly troublesome," muttered Xophnius reproachfully. "*Needlessly troublesome...*" A knock at the door sounded unexpectedly from outside, though neither of them took their eyes from each other.

"Xophnius?" came a female's voice. "Are you there?"

"If only you had wisdom to match your courage, friend," Xophnius said and walked to the door. Opening it, he welcomed Nora into the tensely quiet room, which was feeling dark and stuffy at the moment.

"Well, you are heaps better, that is clear," Nora said obliviously as she crossed the room to Fen and glanced over his bandages. Turning to Xophnius she said, "You are marvelous, sir."

"Do not think of it, child," Xophnius replied vaguely and strode across the room, clearly pre-occupied, with his hands held prayer-like up to his lips.

Nora began to notice the uneasy air of the room but turning from Fen she followed Xophnius with her gaze, "On the contrary, sir, I've thought of you nearly all the night. I thought you a kindly hermit yesterday, but I have not come with the same thinking today."

Xophnius turned to her with a strange expression, a sort of curious light flickering in his eyes. "You and I must find time to talk all about that. But at the moment, I have work that must be done."

"Talk about what?" Fen asked, feeling he'd missed something significant.

Ignoring his question, Nora nodded to Xophnius, "I trust you to tell me when we might."

"Might what?" Fen pressed with growing confusion, "What's going on?"

Xophnius answered Fen with a smile, "In time. Your friend is perceptive and has questions to be answered. We are alike in that. But first, the work of the day. The himbus roots are ripe and must be gathered if my horse is to be fed."

"I would be grateful to help you," offered Fen.

But Xophnius shook his head, "Not quite yet. If you are to return home this evening, you'll need the day to rest. I'm sure Nora is suited to watch over you till I return."

"Sir, I assure you I feel strength at least equal to the labor," said Fen.

"No doubt you do. Strength is not what you lack," replied Xophnius. "You'll see to him, dear?" he asked Nora.

She nodded a smile to Xophnius and watched him then exit to the swamp beyond.

"Well, that was all very strange and confusing," Fen said matter-of-factly to Nora.

"Was it?"

"You always find such satisfaction in knowing things that I don't," said Fen with a disapproving tone.

"I always find satisfaction in knowing things that matter," she corrected in a good-natured way. "That you do not know them is your own business."

And so they spent the next many hours passing the time with easy conversation and one longish nap for Fen, and a meal of sorts—if you consider a crusty piece of brown bread and a pear to be a meal. They left the door open for whatever fresh air the swamp was able to give, and Nora busied herself with a bit of cleaning—the washing of dishes and trimming of lamp wicks, sweeping the floors and filling the water basin from the well outside.

"You ought to let me cut your hair," Nora said

casually at one point in the afternoon. She had been eyeing Fen's brown mop that had grown a bit shaggy for her liking. "We have nothing better to do, and it's obviously been a while since you've seen to it."

Fen raked his long fingers through his rowdy locks. "While I so deeply appreciate your great kindness in such an offer," he began. Fen swung his legs down from the bench where he had been lying and sat, facing Nora with a playfulness hiding just beneath his resolute facade. "And though it grieves me to disappoint you, I believe I shall forego the scenario you suggest in which you come anywhere near my head with any tool that is remotely sharp."

Nora put her hands on her hips and sighed. "How long, Fen? It has been at least…"

He cocked his head and raised his eyebrows, questioning how she would finish the sentence. She held her tongue.

"Yes?" he prompted. "How long has it been since you nearly cut off my ear in your kindly attempt to make me more presentable?"

Nora crossed her arms and huffed at a strand of her own hair. "You know I felt awful about that."

"As did I."

"We were *children* then. It was ages ago. I would think—," Nora argued, but Fen interrupted.

"I no more wish to lose an ear at twenty then I did at twelve, thank you."

Nora dropped the matter. Turning back to the small kitchen area, she grabbed the kettle she had cleaned earlier and put it back in an empty spot on the shelf just above her head.

"I hope my offensively long hair will in no way keep you from thinking me the handsomest Winn you know," Fen said after a few moments of silence.

A slight high-pitched "ha" escaped her lips before Nora quite realized it. She continued busying herself with work, hoping that he would not notice.

Fen lowered himself back down to the couch. "I heard that you know."

She smiled at that, though she said nothing. And she smiled again when she heard him murmuring, "I mean, I suppose I said it to make you laugh... but on second thought... never mind."

It was nearly evening, when they heard Xophnius returning and went out to meet him. He dragged a wooden raft-like object behind him, which was piled high with large roots that resembled potatoes without their skins. He wore a very pleased look, and his hair hung wet with sweat about his face. Upon seeing the two of them he began to call out, but the next moment all of their attention was shifted.

A large hawk flew towards them—strangely, as if heading directly and intentionally for them. Fen and Nora were amazed to see the bird, in fact, alight on a branch just near where Xophnius had halted. He began a series of sounds that could be best described as whistlings and clickings, to which Xophnius paid very close attention. After a long final note, the man stroked the hawk's breast feathers, and the bird launched into easy flight with his powerful wings and was gone.

Fen and Nora stood in speechless wondering. When Xophnius finally spoke, his feelings were evident.

"Unthinkable! Thundering Horsemen of Elethas, how dare they!"

Fen was the first to question. "What has happened? And how in the Four Corners—," he started.

"I have lived a long time on this weary earth, and to think I have lived long enough to see an Elder refused by his own. Of all the—!" Xophnius was beside himself.

"Then it's true—you *are*," said Nora.

"What's true?" Fen asked.

"Precisely," Xophnius answered Nora, "though I don't know what it's worth in this hour."

"I haven't any idea what we're talking about," Fen stressed.

"Xophnius is an Elder. He is one of the five," answered Nora reverently.

Fen looked carefully at his friend to judge her seriousness. Then he looked carefully at Xophnius, who stood tremulous with indignation. Looking back to Nora, he said slowly and deliberately, "I think it's time we leave."

Nora gave a pleading shake of her head, but Xophnius answered, "Indeed we will have to leave. Unfortunately, we will be making the long journey to Kysmarc. On the bright side there will be feasting in abundance, as is always the case with those irresponsible gluttons. Let us make preparations—we'll need leave in the morning."

4

SECRETS IN THE NORTH

You will not be surprised to hear that Fen in no way supported the idea of traveling with Xophnius to Kysmarc and was utterly bewildered that the man should suggest the thing. Likewise, it may be easily guessed that Nora was rather in favor of following the man's instructions however unusual and unfounded they might have seemed.

Grable had been strangely encouraging of the venture, when Fen arrived late that night with Nora and Xophnius both. They had all talked for an hour or so, with Xophnius requesting time to confer privately with Grable for nearly another full hour. And when Grable finally looked at Fen after all had been said and instructed him to take Storm because she was the strongest and fastest of their horses—born on the very night of the greatest storm in a century—well, something in Fen knew that the trip was a thing that, for some inexplicable reason, must be done.

Nora's father had said absolutely no, and her mother had said absolutely yes. And as she was 18 years of age which was entirely two years past the Winn rite of adulthood, she made up her mind quite easily that she would join the ride to Kysmarc. Her mother would lead the students' lessons for the week, which was, as you may have sensed from the little you already know, a thing very much like her mother would do.

But these late night discussions on this particular

night are not the only ones of significance for us. Far to the north and east, in the land of Dresdor, other conversations of extreme importance were taking place in dark corners behind closed doors.

Of the tribe's many great cities, Valdestria is the Principal City of Dresdor. Its cobbled streets weave a maze of both gentle curves and sharp angles, an intricate web extending in every direction with shops and grand homes and businesses lining all of them on both sides.

Once upon a time, long before the age of industry and progress, Valdestria had been the home of Kembarius the True; and the idea of royal dominion had never quite worked its way out of Dresden thinking.

On this late spring night, the street lamps were lit up with the warm glow of candles, their light bouncing off the stones of the streets and casting an illumined haze amid the dark buildings. Few people were to be seen out of doors, for the hour was late. Window shades were drawn and all was quiet, as was usually the case in Dresden cities after dark. One might even be inclined to think the nights had grown too quiet as of late. For there is one quiet that is peaceful rest, and there is another that is uneasy caution. And nighttime in Dresdor seemed to be marked more by the latter.

Through the unnervingly empty Valdestria streets a young man walked briskly, trying to measure his steps quietly. A black cloak flowed long, and a high collar was turned up, covering most of his pale face. The brim of his hat curled down almost to meet the upturned collar, so that there was very little of the actual man to be seen at all.

He glanced occasionally over his shoulder for any evidence that he might be under someone's watchful eye. At the next crossing he turned sharply left down a street with a number of impressive homes on either side, dark ornamental gates looming up eerily in the misty glow of night.

He fixed his eyes on the largest of the houses down on the right at the end of the lane and took a breath. Almost there. A sound from behind startled him, the sound as of a bit of metal scraping something hard. He spun around and looked sharply from side to side. There was nothing to be seen, nothing to be heard. Perhaps it had merely been a rat out seeking its dinner.

Waiting a moment more and seeing nothing, the man satisfied himself that he was not being followed and turned briskly, aiming once again for the stately residence at the end of the street.

He was there a minute later, rapping quietly on the gate of dark polished wood. An exquisitely crafted crest of copper and silver was fixed to the panel, signifying the House of Dresbane. He was let in silently the next moment. And by the time he had crossed the front garden and reached the main entrance of the house, the front door opened to him and he slipped inside.

"Pertius," spoke a young man from the shadows of the unlit house, "how has the night unfolded?"

The late night visitor answered. "They are meeting, Sabian. I followed one of them to the inn just behind the Parliament House. There are at least twelve in one of the upper rooms."

"Have you told Huros?" asked the man in the shadows called Sabian.

"No, I have come first to you."

Sabian nodded. "You must find him. I go now to see what I can learn. Bring Huros and meet me at the inn."

"Sabian, you cannot think to go there alone," Pertius urged.

"If we do not stop the Norians, friend, we shall lose far more than we can afford. I will be careful. Go."

Without a further word, Pertius slipped back out into the night. A few moments behind him, out came Sabian, a hooded cloak shrouding him in darkness.

Twenty minutes had passed before Sabian came to the wide avenue on which the Parliament House is situated. Turning east on it, he kept as close to the buildings and out of the lamp light as possible. Just before reaching the perimeter of the parliament grounds, he turned right onto a narrow alley that ran behind them. Dodging behind buildings and between walls, Sabian eventually found himself at the steps to the back entrance of the Mooncourt Inn.

Sharpening his eyes on the windows above, he spied one that seemed to house the dim glow of candlelight inside. He crept up the stairs and reached for the cold brass door knob. Locked. He glanced rapidly up and down the alley, urgently looking for a way inside. He dared not risk being noticed at the main welcome. And then he caught sight of something high up and realized he had his plan.

Half a block down stood a pub with a staircase running up its back wall to a rooftop dining courtyard. He was up the stairs in a flash and carefully making his way back towards the inn atop the roofs of the adjoining buildings. Reaching a low stone chimney top, Sabian sat with his back to it and his ear pressed to cool smooth stone. A low murmur of voices floated up from the room below.

"We do not have the vote yet," said one man.

"No," said another, "we are close but several are holding out. And changing their minds is proving impossible."

A few other voices expressed agreement, followed by one man who said, "And we have already pushed hard, perhaps too hard. The stubborn ones are growing suspicious."

Again there were murmurs agreeing and then another voice—altogether different from the previous ones. It was deeper, harsher; and it bit through the hum of the other voices like a knife might cut twine in one strong single hack.

"No!"

Even Sabian flinched slightly, startled by the voice.

"If I wanted men of fear I would have given the job to slaves. We have been waiting for the vote to war, and we are now tired of waiting. Either you can secure the war resolution or you cannot. And if you cannot..." there was a pause, "I do not think you want me to entertain that option."

The first voice spoke up nervously, "You will have it, Kaineaux, you will have it. It's that Dresbane and the party that follows him. But we will manage them."

A soft bird-like whistle sounded from the streets, and Sabian peered over the ledge of the inn to see what he knew to be Pertius and Huros in the shadow of the buildings across the street. But before he could signal to them, he heard the menacing voice of Kaineaux again.

"Who knows you are here?" he demanded.

"Nobody," was muttered by a series of stammering voices.

"Nobody," Kaineaux's voice repeated. "Fools! You are watched here."

Sabian heard a blade unsheathed and the door to the room open. He looked feverishly at the wide-open roofscape around him, figuring on which direction he should make for.

Presently, the back door of the Mooncourt Inn was thrust open, and a giant of a man stepped out into the night. Everything about him, from his skin to his jerkin to his wickedly carved blade, blended seamlessly into the dark. His cruel eyes penetrated every crevice and corner of the alley, but he found nothing. It was empty, and it remained empty, all curious eyes and ears having stolen away into the labyrinth of city streets and disappeared.

5

A TENTATIVE ALLIANCE

At the earliest moments of dawn Xophnius, Fen, and Nora set off on the winding dirt road that led eastward across Winderlawk. Fen was insistent that it did *not* mean he believed all this business about Xophnius being an Elder. Neither did it mean he was committed to everything the man might ask of him. And there were a multitude of other such qualifications Fen stressed, that the other two found understandable and tiring at the same time.

The sunrise was before them and the quiet countryside of Winderlawk piling up behind them more with every passing hour. Their destination in Kysmarc was the mountain village of Ildiys; and they would make it by the afternoon of the third day Xophnius had said, if the weather held fair and they did not encounter any unforeseen delays.

It must also be mentioned that these three riders were not the only to ride out from Winderlawk this day. A careful distance behind our travelers rode a band of four, bound also for the higher grounds of the Kysmen. Their firm resolve was that they should go unnoticed, which, as you will see, was to prove ultimately impossible.

The first day passed pleasantly enough. Only when the sun was at its peak did the companions feel just slightly warmer than comfortable. When once the sun was at their back they actually quite enjoyed themselves. For despite Fen's initial reluctance, he could not help feel a wild, exhilarating stir to be leaving his homeland to venture through land he had only heard of. Nora was, of course, delighted for such an opportunity to be in the company of someone so intriguing and venerable as Xophnius. And he, in turn, was always the better for getting out of the thickness of the swamp and into open country. It had actually made him rather high-spirited.

They bantered back and forth throughout the afternoon with Fen reckoning that he ought to at least learn what he might from their leader (or perhaps more accurately *about* their leader).

"Why the Lawksbur, Xophnius? I shouldn't think a swamp the most sensible place for an Elder."

Xophnius's response had simply been, "Precisely."

"How long have you lived there?" Fen then asked. "The house doesn't seem particularly old, and as I understand you've been around for… an unusually long time."

Xophnius smiled. "'*Unusually long time.*' I've had blocks of cheese an 'unusually long time,'" he said and shook his head. "I am older than age."

Nora pressed him, "But were you born in Winderlawk? I asked you when we met as we walked to your camp and you said—"

Xophnius interrupted, "I am older than Winderlawk. There was no such name when I was first given mine, because there was no such thing."

The road was winding with a gradually steeper pitch through larger hills as they drew nearer to the border between the two tribes. Pine trees, were beginning to dot the landscape. Nora had seen them in a book once, but they were a new sight for Fen.

Xophnius's deep voice continued, "I feel as if I am from all the Four Corners of the Earth, though in answer to your curiosity, I was *first* from the land that does indeed belong now to Winderlawk. I then spent several years in the woods to the north (which is Ahlred now) under the tutelage of a great man who lived there. And then of course when I was in the court of the King, we were situated in what is present Dresdor. All the in-betweenings from one place to another will be of little interest to you. And in the ages since then I have wandered the Western Wastes and mapped the Northern Plains, crossed the Southern Deserts and battled the Barbarians of the Eastern Realms. The world beyond the Four Corners is no place for man. Let me assure you."

Fen and Nora both sensed a heaviness growing in his tone, and neither was quite sure how to proceed. Nora ventured to say that she was familiar with his Writings, that in particular his *Letter from Bolkahn* had been very profound to her and full of both wisdom and hope. She *wished* she might have also felt the freedom to ask what the Battle of Bolkahn had been like and a dozen other questions that came to her mind. But she felt it more prudent to leave such questions for another time.

Xophnius murmured to himself at Nora's words and then brought his horse to a full stop. He stared up quietly into the stony hills for a long time before turning back to his company and fixing his gaze intently on Nora. "Child, I cannot recall the last time I spoke to someone who had read the Writings of the Elders. Nor can I recall the last time I heard the word "Bolkahn" spoken. It is as if someone has walked in a bit of my own history and now shares in the memory with me." His voice grew just the slightest bit thick. "You cannot imagine. I thank you."

With that he fell back into a trot, and the three traveled on in silence. When they finally stopped for the night well after dark, Nora found herself more fatigued than she had expected. She lay down to rest her sore back as the men began to take their rations out of their packs, and she was asleep before they had even glanced her direction.

Fen and Xophnius each quietly ate a few bites of dried meat and a biscuit before unrolling their blankets and settling in for the night. As he looked up at the sky, Fen thought the stars looked especially brilliant from this particular spot. And he felt the wild stirring again. It was more than the powerful sensation of simply beholding something vast—as it is when one tries to take in something as immense as the Sea or the Sky and in doing so feels most keenly his own smallness. No, this stirring moved beyond that. It was an awakening of something churning deep inside, but for the life of him he could not name it—this mysterious yearning and anticipation.

"Xophnius?" he asked softly.

"Yes."

"I suppose at some point you'll tell me why I am here... and what this whole strange business is about?"

It was quiet for a beat before Xophnius replied, "Precisely."

On the morning of the second day of their journey, the companions came to the River Marcs, which runs generally north to south separating Winderlawk from Kysmarc. It flows out of the greatest of all the rivers in the Four Corners, the Medius. That great river travels all the way from the edge of the Western Wastes, dividing the northern and southern tribes, till it reaches the border with the Eastern Realms and carries on still further to the Lost Sea.

Emptying into the Medius from the far Northern Plains, and so dividing Ahlred (in the west) from Dresdor (in the east) is the smallest of the three primary rivers, the River Mullen. Thus are the tribal boundaries clearly defined by these three aquatic arteries.

Reaching the River Marcs invigorated all three riders, and they paused for a moment at the great stone bridge with its pillared arches reaching far down into the rough, rocky waters below. This stage of the river was a breathtaking spot, as it coursed vigorously through the channel it had forged over centuries. The mountains were steep on either side, blanketed heavily with moss and ferns of various kinds. Roads from both the south and north of Winderlawk converged here with the road taken by our three travelers.

"Well, friends," said Xophnius, "as the poet Velayne has penned:

> *The glory of the river is to rend and run;*
> *yet 'tis mastered by the bridge*
> *that has challenged it-*
> *and won."*

The clop of hoofs on the bridge was by far drowned in the noise of the surging river below them.

"Have you ever seen anything this beautiful?" Nora asked Fen in a sort of hushed and whispered reverence.

Fen shook his head slightly, taking in the surrounding majesty, "No, Nora. Never."

They traveled on from the bridge, making their way along a series of switchbacks that cut a pass through the mountain. The pass crossed over to a wide valley, where the road stretched straight for what appeared to be a few miles. They had only just reached the tall valley grasses when Xophnius's mare pulled up and started to stamp her front right hoof angrily. Her ears twitched and she tossed her head wildly, setting the other horses uneasy. Fen and Nora went immediately to soothing their steeds, but Xophnius lifted eyes of an eagle to the countryside on their right, where near a dozen mounted riders could be seen scattered in the distance.

They wore brown hooded masks and each wielded a

sword of an unusually darker metal—nothing like Fen had ever seen before; and they were unmistakably watching the three.

Fen had quickly noticed Xophnius's response and saw the band of threatening strangers. He glanced at Nora, who was still unaware of the situation and then looked swiftly to Xophnius for instruction.

Keeping an unwavering eye on the band of horsemen, Xophnius spoke to Fen in a low voice, "You must ride with Nora. You must fly all the way to Ildiys."

"Absolutely not," Fen snapped in a fierce whisper. "I'll not leave you here to face ten men."

Nora looked up quickly, caught by surprise at Fen's tone. Then she finally saw what Xophnius was watching.

"Who are they?" she asked in a frantic whisper.

Xophnius did not acknowledge her question but responded sharply and urgently to Fen, "You must do exactly as I say. Their horses are swift—chargers from the north. They will push you to the brink. You have no speed to spare if you expect to get her to safety."

"Xophnius!" Fen argued. But just as he spoke the name, the gray mare neighed violently and reared, for the hooded riders were on the move.

"Go!" roared Xophnius, swiping his sword from the sheath slung across his back. The blade was brilliant in the sunlight, and the mare leaped to the gallop with Xophnius bent over her neck. His right arm stretched straight towards the ground behind him with the sword extending like lightening from his hand. He was a streak of fury charging like a warrior.

At Xophnius's command Fen had yelled for Nora to hold on and grabbed for his leather whip. With a fierce shout he whipped Nora's horse, setting her into a wild gallop and set Storm at a fierce chase just behind.

Nora's thoughts and fears were raging. *Elethas, keep*

us. Behind her, Fen was thundering on Storm shouting the cries of the Winn horsemen and urging the horses faster, faster. He dared not look back, and yet he was sick inside to leave a man to fight so many alone. He would find a safe place for Nora, and he would go back. On the horses raced.

Behind them Xophnius was just a few moments from reaching his target. Several of the riders had turned his direction and were heading to meet his challenge. But at least six held swift pursuit after Fen and Nora.

Xophnius gave a thunderous shout as he prepared to meet the foremost of the riders. His sword was raised now, and as the two men came to the point of meeting he struck with deadly speed. The opposing swordsmen was thrown from his seat, and Xophnius charged on ferociously with scarcely a loss of momentum.

Two were coming at him evenly now, with a third just a breath behind. He looked from rider to rider, assessing the order of his attack and reached with his left hand for the knife that was cased at his thigh. But even as he drew it, he saw a change come over the riders. They started to wildly pull up their panting horses and turn to flee, but two white feathered arrows whizzed past Xophnius and landed in the chests of the first two riders. The third rider had turned and was in full flight when a third arrow shot him through the back, and he slumped off his horse to the ground.

Xophnius spared no time to stop and see what other party had entered the conflict. He corrected his course and made a mad break for the six who still hounded Fen and Nora—and who were visibly gaining ground. He leaned down over the horse's ear and spoke something, and the mare responded with a surge of power and a torrent of speed.

What Xophnius could not see behind him were the

four riders who had followed them from Winderlawk, who were now pounding across the valley towards the same target as he. And, of course, none of this was known to Fen and Nora who were near reaching the far edge of the valley now and racing to keep their advantage.

Fen risked a glance at his pursuers and saw that they had closed in significantly. "Go, Nora!" he shouted and drew his whip again across the backside of her horse. But no speed was gained from the poor horse, for there was truly no possible speed to be gained.

"Fen!" Nora shouted. Keeping her eyes fixed ahead she saw with horror, as the grasses parted, that the road leading out of the valley and up through the steep hills was blocked. A mass of rock and limbs had slid from one of the hill sides and lay piled and scattered about for some distance. Their way of escape lay miserably beneath it.

Fen saw and let out a yell of rage. "Ride in carefully and take whatever way you can!" he shouted to her.

"What? Where are you going!" she reigned in her spent beast just slightly and frantically turned in her seat to see him.

He had already pulled up and turned to face the oncoming attackers. "I'm holding them off. Ride!"

"No!!" she yelled with all the force she could command.

"Ride, Nora—now!"

She knew she must and let out something like a scream that swelled for the anger and fear and exhaustion she felt. She turned quickly to the coming hills and looked for what might be a crossable route. Seeing what appeared to be a possible gap, she headed out of the valley left of her original course as swiftly as she was able.

Meanwhile, Fen sat on his mount and watched the grassy horizon, his eyes keen and sharp, his sword drawn and at the ready. There was a slight rise in the valley they had just come over, and so the distance he could now see looking back that direction was tragically short. They would be over the rise at any moment, how many he did not know. He guessed that Xophnius had taken care of several of them. At best he would still be outnumbered, at worst... terribly outnumbered.

His blood coursed through his body like thunder, and his hand gripped the hilt of his sword with a hold like death. The grasses swayed gently in the vale's breeze. Still no riders.

His heart pounded in his chest, and he forced himself a slow measured breath, steeling himself for battle. Still no riders. His senses grew sharp, and he listened. Storm stood easy—that is, recovering from her race but not tense as with an oncoming charge.

And then there were riders. But they were not the brown hooded men. It was Xophnius and four others. Three men and a single woman rode round him all on white, lean horses with bows strung at their backs. There was a tense silence between the five as they came over the rise; but when Fen saw them he felt a flood of relief, and the taut muscles of his body relaxed.

"Aegius!" he shouted to the man who rode at Xophnius's right.

Aegius was a man of thirty. He had black, straight hair and keen blue eyes that took in everything. His face was long and at Fen's call, a smile broke out through his short dark beard.

"Hello, friend. The raiders are spent; you may be easy," Aegius called back.

Over the next immediate minutes Nora was reached, and the group gathered at a spot up the hill a bit where they would see well anyone who might come. And they rested.

Xophnius wore the sternest of expressions, and the new foursome seemed also reserved. But Fen and Nora were glad beyond words, for the four were friends.

"Xophnius, this is Aegius Fotterhil. These are his brothers—Liam and Khaz, and his sister—Wylla," Fen properly introduced the four to the grave man who neither nodded nor spoke but simply observed in serious fashion.

Aegius looked the older man dead in the eye for some time; then he spoke. "We trouble you. You need not explain it. I understand your concern."

The tension was perplexing to Fen and Nora, the latter of whom spoke up saying, "I don't understand. The four of you just came to our rescue, did you not? Why not let's celebrate the joyous providence that saw fit to cross our paths in such an hour of need? Thank you."

She looked back and forth helplessly between Xophnius who stood on the one hand and Aegius who stood facing him with his brothers and sister just behind.

"Why were you coming into the Valley of Shaw on this hour of this day?" Xophnius questioned firmly.

"We were following you, sir," Aegius responded plainly.

"That is obvious. Why?"

"I cannot say now, but we will speak openly when we reach the council in Ildiys," said Aegius.

"*When we reach the...*" muttered Xophnius in astonishment. "What in the Four Corners makes you think you will travel with us to Ildiys or that you have any place in a council there!" he thundered.

Fen and Nora listened in bewilderment as the two men went back and forth.

"I understand, Xophnius. I must say that I know more about you than you would wish, but we are not enemies, you and I," Aegius offered.

"What you know of me could not fill an ink well. And I will determine if you are my enemy," the man replied.

Fen interjected at this point, stepping between the two and pointing to Aegius, "He is not an enemy. I have known him all my life. He is a friend," he entreated Xophnius, "*I know him.*"

"And you will know me even better soon, Fen," said Aegius, "but for now, Xophnius, we may as well all agree to be companions. Though we may not yet be friends, we have slain a number of your enemies which should at least separate us from their status in your eyes. And what's more we are going to the same place; you cannot avoid that by traveling separately."

Xophnius's reservations were not at all abated, but he saw the fixedness of the situation and agreed that they might travel together with the understanding that he would be forced to slay them all were they to give him the slightest reason. And on that note, they struck out at an easy walking pace (for the moment) headed for the mountain village of Ildiys.

6

AN UNIMAGINED FORCE

It was a tired and silent company that arrived at the iron gates of Kholrihk's palatial home on the evening of the following day. From outside the perimeter they heard the fluid melodies of an ensemble of musicians floating lazily in the dusky air, along with the faint sounds of pleasant conversation. You may be sure that the gathering in the garden struck a different tone altogether when the gardener opened the gates and our party entered with Xophnius at the lead.

"Kholrihk!!" shouted Xophnius. He had dismounted along with the others and was making straight for one man and two women who had been chatting gaily in the center of the garden. The musicians ceased their song in one awkward, instantaneous moment. All heads turned; all voices quieted.

"Kholrihk!" Xophnius repeated passionately, closing the distance between the large man and himself with long, forceful strides.

Kholrihk held up both arms, palms extended gently against Xophnius. "Come peacefully, brother. Anger is neither a friend nor a help."

"Neither is laziness, you cow," Xophnius shot back. "Can you no longer suffer your grazing here to be interrupted?"

Bryn stepped past Kholrihk and extended her hand to Xophnius, "We are glad you've come, friend. Pax."

Xophnius left her greeting unanswered and stared at

53

the both of them obstinately. Then the other woman came forward. Braving the storm of his temper, she put her arms around Xophnius's neck, kissing him lightly on each cheek and said, "It is wonderful to see you, Xophnius. I am thoroughly delighted."

Her softness brought out something of the same in him, and he reluctantly resigned himself to it. "Hello, Phlycia," he said in a calmer tone, "A long time it has been."

He looked from Phlycia to Bryn to Kholrihk, working at an attempt to keep his demeanor more civilized, and taking a deep breath he asked, "And where is Huros?"

"Huros will come in the morning hour," Kholrihk answered stepping over to his friend and embracing him in the old customary fashion. "But come, tell us who is in your party, and all of you take something to eat. Certainly you have need of it after your journey."

Xophnius nodded and motioned for Fen to join him. "This is the young man, Fen, whom I bring before the council of the Elders. His companion Nora has accompanied us," he added, gesturing her way. "And these four whose identity is little known to me have come from Winderlawk as well for purposes they have been thus far unwilling to communicate."

His statement drew raised eyebrows and expressions of concern and surprise from Kholrihk, Bryn, and Phlycia—whom you have surely known by now to be three of the remaining Elders.

Bryn spoke first, and there was a ring of disapproval in her voice, "That is rather unheard of—presuming to attend a council of the Elders uninvited."

"These days seem to have no lack of unprecedented events," mumbled Xophnius, to which Bryn only sighed.

"We are quite aware of the strangeness of our

presence here," offered Aegius. "But what we have come to share with you we believe you will be most interested in learning."

"You have come to teach us something?" Bryn questioned rather scornfully. Then turning to Xophnius, she asked, "And did you think this acceptable? To bring perfect strangers into our midst when the business at hand is such?"

But Aegius spoke before Xophnius could respond, "Excuse my impudence, madam. He has in no way been agreeable to this strangest of developments. We have forced ourselves shamefully on the council and would not have done so if we had not felt that the future of the kingdom—and one might add, your mission—were not in the balance."

His words hung uncomfortably over the group for a moment, and then he added, "We will, of course, sleep outside with the horses and expect nothing from you but the chance to speak plainly with you in the morning."

Kholrihk, who had been studying the man carefully since he had begun speaking, answered, "You are welcome to dine with us and to rooms inside the house for the night, for if I know anything from my years on this earth, I know you are not a man of treachery."

Aegius and his siblings nodded in respectful acceptance.

Phlycia had been watching Fen, studying the dark of his eyes, the strength of his jaw, the square of his shoulders. She had marked the good-natured and yet intense way he had about him, and she now asked, "What is your family name, son?"

"I don't know, madam," he answered plainly, "I never knew them."

His words seemed to take the Elders aback (excepting Xophnius, of course), and their astonishment unnerved Fen a bit. It was Xophnius who answered Phlycia, saying simply, "Just because he did not know his parents does not mean he did not have any, now does it?"

Fen and Nora exchanged questioning looks, but the Elders seemed ready to suspend all further business till the morning. Kholrihk insisted that they all fill their glasses and their plates until they should be heartily satisfied, and there was quite a more hopeful and easy spirit about the group when heads were finally laid to pillows late that night.

Morning came with a rush of gorgeous colors that painted the sky in hues of peaches and nectarines. The mountain air was fresh and crisp, and the smell of gardenias haunted the place as every room and hall seemed to have a cluster of them adorning a delicate pitcher or floating in a silver basin.

The hall where the Elders were to gather was a towering room on the fourth floor (the highest level of the house). It had a high vaulted ceiling and long, narrow windows that spanned nearly the entire height of the walls. A large but not enormous table sat in the center of the room. Its base was of thick dark wood, and its top made of polished white stone which caught the light from the windows with perfect balance, lighting the entire room with a clear, gentle brightness. Ten elegantly carved chairs sat around the table, two at the ends and four on each side.

The group that assembled at first in the room was large. There was, of course, the company of the previous night which made eleven persons; and they were joined by two more this morning. One was the fifth Elder, Huros; the other, a young man with somewhat shortly cropped blond hair and fine features. He wore a tailored tunic with stiff collar, braided belt, fine boots—which is to say, his dress was the sharp and sophisticated style of Dresdor. Several eyed the young stranger with a subtle and quiet curiosity, and finally Kholrihk called for everyone's attention.

"Friends," he began, "this is a most unusual council. But as this is the road that has been laid for us, let us take it as it comes. May I suggest that the Elders be permitted time alone to confer, after which we may attend to matters in due course."

With no objection, the various newcomers to council exited the room, and the five Elders took their seats around the table.

"Tell us why we are here, Xophnius," Kholrihk began. "You have our ear."

"Do you remember the young woman of high interest to me some years ago? Westerlyn Lawk was her name. She lived on a farm in Ainsworth with her husband Grable."

The members around the table nodded their heads.

"Twenty years ago, perhaps?" Kholrihk supposed.

"Precisely," said Xophnius. "I had followed a chain of outstanding evidences that had led me very nearly to believe she was of the royal bloodline."

"The poor woman died young, did she not?" asked Phlycia.

"Yes. She grew ill, though with what disease I do not know. It was said that she was taken to a healer in the north. And she did not return."

"Many, Xophnius, have been of high interest to you only to disappoint," spoke Bryn with a cool edge to her voice.

"Let him speak," Huros broke in, "for he does not come simply to draw up old memories."

Xophnius continued, "Five days ago I came to the aid of the young man and woman who have journeyed here with me. Fen was injured fairly seriously, and I treated him at my camp. In the course of our conversation, I learned that he was abandoned as an orphan at Grable Lawk's door, no less than the same year his wife had passed on."

"What is your thought, brother?" asked Kholrihk.

"My thought? Well, to begin, I think it strange for the man's wife to be away some months and then for a baby to arrive on his very steps," answered Xophnius. "I think it strange that so very little was said of her condition or of her passing. I think it all very strange beyond coincidence."

"You think him the son of Westerlyn?" asked Bryn. "And what of his mother then? If she went away to have a baby where is she?" Her eyes gleamed with a challenging spark, and her voice held an imperious tone.

Xophnius shook his head, "No doubt she did die, perhaps in childbirth. But why should an infant be abandoned to this widower if there were not some compelling connection?"

"I agree the circumstances seem suspicious," began Huros, "but we are a long way yet from an heir. Firstly, you were not able to confirm the woman's identity. What is more, it does not seem we can confirm the boy's identity any better. Besides, if he were the man's son, as you suspect, why the pretense? It does not seem to me very promising."

"He has the stance of Kembarius, have none of you thought it?" Phlycia's gentle voice rang out with a warm and commanding energy.

"It struck me so, Phlycia, yes," replied Xophnius.

"So then," asked Kholrihk, "have you spoken to the boy about it?"

"Certainly not," Xophnius replied with firmness. "It is far too early for that. The less he knows—until the time is right—the safer he will be. Certainly time and history have taught us that much."

"And why does he think he is here?" Bryn asked.

"He awaits the answer," said Xophnius. "I suspect he was only willing to come at all because Grable encouraged it. I spoke with him the night before we traveled."

"Did you question him outright about the boy?" asked Huros.

"I dared not," replied Xophnius. "If he does not know the boy's true identity it would risk overwhelming him with far too much at one time. On the other hand, if he does know, he has obviously worked to keep the boy's identity a secret. To expose it would risk threatening his sense of security and possibly sending him with the boy into hiding. We have seen both over the ages, have we not?"

"So what did you say to this man?" asked Bryn.

"I spoke along other lines, which are equally true and pressing. I spoke of the darkness that has been creeping into Winderlawk and the dangers that are lurking at its borders. I said plainly enough that I sensed in Fen someone with the strength to stand for Winderlawk and help lead the tribe through its dark days. He conceded to let him come... to my thought, because he knows he is the rightful ruler and must begin to take his place."

"Or because you play to a man's ego," challenged Bryn, "who imagines the boy riding the glories of victory he himself desires. This is a fantasy far-fetched, Xophnius, even for you."

Kholrihk held up his hands, calling for a halt. "Your feelings are plainly read by all, Bryn. We each one may have our questions, but what is your proposal, Xophnius?"

"We have learned that this task of finding a king—

and what is more, crowning a good king—is a disastrously delicate business. I would like to keep him with me, for a time. Observe him. Mentor him... open his eyes to the threats and schemes that Ahmahnric is working against the people of the Four Corners. If my intuitions are correct, he may find his own way to the throne."

The other Elders did not seem to have any objections to what Xophnius said. And he added, in a somewhat reprimanding manner, "Of course, I would expect this council's aid to be immediate and sure if I were to call for it."

Before Bryn had the chance to voice her opinion about his last words, Kholrihk answered, "That is fair, friend. You shall have it if it is needed."

It was decided, next, to call for the four riders of Winderlawk and learn what their business was. Thus when they had been summoned to their places at the table, the council continued. Xophnius briefly relayed to the Elders the surprising presence of the four in the Valley of Shaw, their quick riding and skill with the bow, and their unexplained insistence on joining the gathering in Ildiys. When asked to share their errand with the council, Aegius stood quietly with a respectful bow of his head and began his tale.

"Fine men and women, I must share things with you that, I fear, you will find most difficult to hear. They are equally difficult to confess, and I ask from the beginning for your mercy and pardon. Though you count us as strangers, I must admit that you are not at all strangers to us."

A thick silence filled the room, a stillness of intense attention. Five sets of penetrating eyes were fastened on the man who spoke; they missed nothing. Aegius held himself with a noble humility and continued on, "My name is Aegius Fotterhil. Of my brothers who remain there are Liam and Khaz." He gestured to each of them and then placed a hand on the shoulder of his sister who sat next to him. "Our sister is Wylla. We belong to a certain Order, an Order that has existed longer than you may believe. Its identity and purpose has been a secret kept with the strongest lock. That I am disclosing these things to you today breaks an oath that was centuries kept and sealed with the blood of my kinsmen."

Aegius paused for just a moment, readying himself for the rest of what he must say. Suspense lingered uneasily over the table.

"Noble gentlemen and ladies, we are called the Watch. And so has our family been throughout the history of the Four Corners."

Bryn, who could no longer hold silent, asked outright, "Watchers of what?"

"Of the heir of Kembarius, madam," said Aegius.

"For what purpose?" asked Huros.

Aegius's reply was straightforward, "To keep him from you, sir."

7

HEAVY THINGS

Now, when the Elders had announced they would hold private council initially, the others had all ventured down stairs and out into the gardens. Fen and Nora had hoped to spend their time talking with Aegius and his siblings. So they had been slightly disappointed when the four went off alone to have what appeared to be very serious and rather uninterruptible conversation amongst themselves.

The well-dressed late-comer to the residence had immediately gone off by himself as well, clearly uninterested in making the acquaintance of the others. This was only to be expected, since relationship between people of one tribe and another was virtually nonexistent. The feelings of people towards those of the other tribes did not often run on the warm side. This was especially true when it came to Dresdor and any other tribe. For the Ahlrik and the Kysmen and the Winn felt that the Dresden looked down on all the rest as woefully inferior. And they felt so because—in large part—it was so. All this to say, one would not have bargained on a fast friendship with the stranger.

This left Fen and Nora to themselves; and they wandered aimlessly around the tranquil setting, mulling over the puzzling events of the last few days and occasionally voicing a thought or a question for the other to answer.

"Do you wonder why he brought you here?" she

asked.

"How could I not?" Fen replied. "Things have been so different since the mastid storm. I feel as though I have stepped into the shoes of a different man, into a life of which I understand so little. Something has changed. Do you sense it?"

Nora was quiet and thoughtful, and all she said was, "Yes."

"I feel I do not know how to make sense of things anymore."

Nora brushed away a tendril of blooming wisteria that was stretching across the walk. She breathed in its fragrance. "Not everything that is true may be seen with your eyes, Fen."

"Meaning what?"

"You have always chided me about my talk of the Elders and Kembarius and the heir." She stopped walking for a moment and looked at him in a way that made Fen feel uneasy for a moment. "But something inside you says it is all true. Does it not?"

He did not answer and found looking into her face difficult.

"You may deny it if you wish," said she, "but I know I am not mistaken."

And then he did find the resolve to look her straight in the eye. "I will not deny what you say... I would never lie to you."

They had returned to ambling thoughtfully 'round the garden till a servant appeared with a crystal bell that he rung, sounding two high and clear notes. He had called for only the four riders, which had left the three to wait again. Whatever prompted him to do so, Fen turned to the stranger and held out his hand, saying, "The lady is Nora, and I am Fen. We are of Winderlawk."

The blond man was caught off guard and paused a

moment out of sheer surprise. Then clasping Fen's hand, he replied with a pleasant, "I am Sabian Dresbane. Of Dresdor."

"I will be glad to know you better, sir," said Fen.

And Sabian, again surprised, replied, "Likewise, friend."

They spoke of mostly inconsequential things. It was the first time in Kysmarc for all of them, and they commented on the land and the weather, the architecture and the vineyard that sprawled from the edge of the garden wall gently down the slope towards a valley. When tea was brought out and it appeared they would be waiting still some time more, the three each took the cups given them and wandered off in their own directions, that they might enjoy a bit of solitude before being called upon. Meanwhile on the fourth floor, a firestorm of questioning was unfolding.

"What is the meaning of this?!" Huros demanded.

"Peace, Huros," said Phlycia, "he has much to say still. Explain yourself." Phlycia looked at Aegius with neither hostility nor peace, rather a grave curiosity. Her silky white hair was pulled loosely back from her smooth skin into a knot near the top of her head, and her gray eyes flashed with a blaze of intrigue.

Aegius spoke. "I will begin at the beginning... when Tsalina was taken—"

"Tsalina!!" thundered Xophnius, "What do you know of Tsalina that you may tell us?! *We were there*, young one!"

"Xophnius," Kholrihk called out, and Xophnius quieted himself with difficulty.

"Yes," continued Aegius, "you were there. And also a man, Lurihk, and his wife Ursiyl. They were also there."

"Lurihk," Huros repeated the name thoughtfully. "One of the house guard was of that name."

"The same, sir," said Aegius. "And he was at his post

the night Ahmahnric's men came for Tsalina. In point of fact, he witnessed the men making away with her and followed behind. He called for help, but his cries went unheard in the noise of the celebrations being held that night. The men who came were more than he could challenge alone, and he feared that if he went for help they would escape completely. By the time the rest of the guard had discovered her missing and were beginning their response, Lurihk had secretly followed the vile scoundrels nearly as far as the River Mullen—"

"This is madness!" exclaimed Xophnius. "To have the event recounted to me as if I did not ride out that very night on my own horse—as if I did not see it all with my own eyes." His voice was trembling with anger.

"Please, sir," Aegius calmly replied, "The riddles that have so long plagued you may be answered, though at the first it may be a bitter pill. Lurihk tracked the men to the river where a boat waited. Two of the guards went on board with the girl, while the rest stayed behind to present a false story to those who would pursue them. They headed north along the river you will remember."

"We overtook them near the ford at Vahlz," Bryn said, recalling the very scenario.

"But the girl was not there, was she," Aegius soberly acknowledged. "She was on a boat heading south on the Mullen. With Lurihk. He had stolen onto the boat secretly, and with that advantage had easily beaten the two kidnappers, whom he threw overboard. Tsalina was in safe keeping."

The Elders sat speechless, thoughts racing back to that catastrophic night. Memories flooded their minds— the wails of Tsalina's mother, the sound of men rushing out on galloping mounts across the dark land, the urgent calls that rang out when the trail had been discovered... the anger and exhaustion when they returned, with no girl.

Now at the table Liam and Khaz sat straight in their chairs with heads up and eyes forward. Only Wylla could not bring herself to meet the gaze of any of them and kept her focus locked on the table of white stone before her.

"Lurihk did not know whether the royal house was safe yet," Aegius continued, "and was concerned that the girl may still be in danger, so he kept her with him, and the two stayed in hiding. Eventually he got word to his wife, and she joined them. Lurihk and Ursiyl were torn by what they should do, for they did not know who could be trusted. They feared that someone in the palace had worked with the traitor to steal the child—perhaps even one of you."

At this both Xophnius and Huros stormed to their feet, and Xophnius pounded his fists on the stone slab, but Aegius spoke swiftly, "Forgive their error. Ahmahnric had turned, and they knew not who else might follow."

"Pax, sirs," said Bryn to the men on their feet. Her voice made every effort at restraint though it was pure steel, "there is more to hear."

Aegius went on, "Lurihk thought to go back privately and speak to Kembarius himself. But the night before he was to leave, Ursiyl had a dream. In her dream she took the girl back to her father, but as they celebrated the child's return, fires broke out across the grounds and consumed everything and everyone. The woman took the dream as a sign that the girl would not be safe, and they resolved to keep watch over her until the time was right."

"What, then? Did they mean to keep her in hiding for the rest of their lives?" asked Kholrihk.

"And they raised up the next generation to do the same, sir," answered Aegius. "I am in the line of those generations. We have never failed to watch over the heir."

"Thundering horsemen of Elethas! You are nigh seven centuries late bringing such news to light," howled Xophnius.

"Then she did not die at Ahmahnric's hand," Phlycia's warm voice flowed and silenced all else.

"No, madam, she did not," Aegius answered.

Tears spilled over, though otherwise Phlycia remained perfectly composed as she looked from Elder to Elder, "We stormed his fortress. We questioned him fiercely; he said he did not have her. You will remember I said he spoke the truth."

"Shall we feel sorry for not believing a traitor?!" Huros asked in disgust.

"I do not weep sadness for Ahmahnric," Phlycia answered Huros. "I weep joy for the girl who escaped him."

Aegius continued, "The Watch have dedicated their lives and often paid with their deaths to keep Kembarius's heir safe. It became a sacred code; some would say even a religion. Over the years there have been but few who thought to put an end to the hiding and restore the heir to the throne as you have been seeking. Each failed painfully." He paused. "Your own efforts have failed, in no small part due to those of my Order who have worked against you through every age and at every turn to keep the heir from being found."

Xophnius left the table at this point and walked to the long windows. He stared out with the tiredest of eyes and the emptiest of feelings. In truth, there are no words for what the man was feeling at the moment.

"It is unthinkable," Huros growled through clenched jaws, "Unpardonable. You wretches!"

"Huros!" Phlycia broke in, "Shall we condemn the man for the sins of his fathers when he has at last righted an ancient wrong?"

"What then?" cried Huros. "You would do nothing?"

Phlycia replied firmly, "Against the first man who has chosen to act nobly in ages? No, I would not do nothing. I would thank him. Though I am outrageously disappointed to have suffered such deception, I would not senselessly punish the one who would set me free with truth."

It was as if time stood still in the room. Each of the five grew somber and introspective, no doubt recalling various episodes of their never-ending quest and wondering how this unknown enemy had thwarted them, how things might have gone differently at this point or that. Perhaps they questioned how they had never perceived it. They sat frozen, considering at long length the unbearable truth.

"What brings you forward now," asked Bryn finally, "after ages of silence?"

"And who is in your keeping?" asked Kholrihk, a question which captured everyone's attention utterly. All eyes lay fixed on Aegius.

"As to your question, lady, my brothers and sister and I do not share the suspicion of our ancestors. We hold deep respect for the Elders. It is long past time you knew, that you might fulfill the call of Elethas," Aegius said with a grieved sincerity of tone. Then turning to Kholrihk, "For your issue, sir, to my thinking you already have some idea who we watch, else the son of Grable and Westerlyn Lawk would not be here."

A spark of life lit in Xophnius's eyes, and he made his way back to the table where all sat pensive, taking in the remarkable revelations that had shaken their world so unexpectedly this morning and yet, that had possibly forged a new way forward. "So then," Xophnius said, with a voice quiet and small, "out of every dark thing…"

The group spoke hours more. Questions were raised and answered. Tempers rose and abated. History was laid bare, and a new thing sprung up. Lunch had long come and passed, and now the air outside was gathering the chill of dusk in the mountains.

"Do you think there is trouble?" Nora asked of the two men, as the three made their way to one of the quiet rooms inside.

"Unquestionably there is trouble," replied Sabian. "I do not know how it is in Winderlawk, but things are not right in Dresdor. And I hear worrisome news of this place as well."

Just then the sound of footsteps and voices began to make its way down the winding staircase, and the three looked up to see the weary group of men and women descending at last.

"Let us dine!" Kholrihk called out, "And put this day to rest behind us." The group filed past Fen, Nora, and Sabian, ushering them along as well towards a great hall whose windows overlooked the gardens. In it the company found several tables set extravagantly with the feast prepared for them—one with dishes of spiced mutton, roasted pheasant and coconut fish, the catch having come from the fresh rivers of Ildiys that morning. Another table held bowls of steaming herbed potatoes, laden skewers of mushrooms with onions and garlic, and platters of chesney cakes (which is something like grated pumpkin, first mixed with nuts and goat cheese, then fried lightly crisp). Blueberry tarts and apple pies, cups of glazed oranges and figs… the provisions were fragrant, dazzling, and plentiful.

They filled their plates and gathered quietly in twos and threes, relieved to mark the end of a very long day. Huros and Sabian ate in one corner, speaking in low tones. Phlycia, Nora, and Wylla gathered by a window, mostly gazing off and strangely saying very little compared to the overwhelming thoughts and feelings that welled up inside each of them. Xophnius beckoned to Fen, who followed him outside. Neither had taken food; neither had the appetite for it.

It was fairly dark outside now. The gardener was at work, lighting torches that neatly adorned the perimeter of the grounds. Xophnius and Fen stood side by side, watching the new flames flicker and dance in the lively breeze that blew that evening. The night was quiet but for the soothing sounds of the fountain bubbling in the corner. Xophnius looked as if he might have aged years in that day. It did not escape Fen's notice, but he was not sure what he may ask and what should be left alone. He kept to himself and waited for the man to speak first.

"The day has been heavy on you," Xophnius finally spoke. Fen nodded. "Though you do not know why. And that is perhaps the most difficult part," he added.

"Yes," answered Fen, "that is it exactly."

Xophnius nodded and let out a great sigh, "We have all borne heavy things today. Tomorrow, friend. You will know at least something tomorrow."

"You look tired, Xophnius."

"I am more tired than can be told," Xophnius answered in a distant manner, "of a sort that will not be mended with sleep." Then he smiled and turned to Fen, willing away the gravity of the day. "There is much to discuss in the morning. After, we ride for Winderlawk as soon as we may. Rest well tonight. You will need the strength."

"We are going back so soon?" Fen asked, surprised.

"The work here is nearly done," Xophnius replied, "and the work that lies ahead does not lie here first. What must be done, Fen, may be more than you imagine and will certainly require more than you would like."

He placed a fatherly hand on Fen's shoulder, looking him straight in the eyes with intense seriousness. "What you must believe in your bones and remember at all costs is that you are the man for it. One far beyond you or I has already decided that. What remains to be seen is how you will stand in the hour chosen for you."

There were a hundred questions racing through Fen's brain as Xophnius spoke, but all of them fell silent before they could escape his lips. All he could do was nod.

As Xophnius turned to go back inside, Fen stopped him. "Xophnius, what was your heavy thing today?"

A glimmer of joy filled those serious eyes as he smiled back at Fen and said, "You are kind to ask, friend. But it must be mine to bear for now."

8

THE RESISTANCE

The following morning dawned bright and clear. The mood was not overly happy in the place, but there was a resolve and an eagerness to finish the business of the council. Several of them had already taken their seats around the table, steaming tea that sent up the aroma of rich spices set before them. Others were making their way in. Liam, Khaz, and Wylla were not needed for the morning's discussions and were heading to the stables to see that the horses were ready for travel. Nora went with them alongside Wylla.

They were a contrasting picture, Wylla and Nora. The one was dressed as her brothers, in dark riding pants into which a simple linen shirt was snugly tucked. The other wore a long, lovely dress of cranberry color with gauzy sleeves of ivory. The one wore an archer's bow on her back, the other her long, brown hair that hung loose down to her waist. But they talked as they exited the house as if they were sisters and understood each other completely.

"Nora," called Xophnius. She turned quickly at the sound of his voice.

"Good morning," she answered, and her pale cheeks dimpled as she smiled at him.

"I would have you join us if you would be so kind," requested the man.

Nora was surprised but happily so. The council had not been anything like what she had hoped. She had found, for the most part, that she understood nothing more of what was going on than when she arrived. Nora had reminded herself that she had come for Fen's sake anyway, but she was still quietly disappointed that such seemingly important matters were being discussed with her so close to it all and yet so left on the outside.

So her eyes lit up just a bit at Xophnius's words as she left her companions and went with him. As they climbed the stairs that lead to the great hall at the top of the house, she shared some of her thoughts with him.

"I was thinking perhaps it was a mistake for me to come," she said. Xophnius listened. "I had just felt that Fen needed me to be here. This is so... it is all such a difficult thing for him... the Elders and Ahmahnric and the history of the tribes... he has never believed it much, you know. Of course, few in Winderlawk really do anymore. They think it myth. Legend. Well, he has believed it more than he has admitted. But I think he is confused perhaps, or just uneasy—I do not know. And anyway, I don't know that I've been anything of a helpful friend to him here. And I was just telling myself that maybe it was my own selfish fascinations that drove me to come in the first place and that I nearly cost you both significantly when we came to that valley. For I know Fen would have stayed and fought with you but felt he could not for my sake. And you were left alone, but for our friends who came when not at all expected. And if I just hadn't come..." she rattled on as fast as she could speak the thoughts. They had nearly reached the top of the stair when she finished, and Xophnius stopped them and turned to her with a warm but strong expression.

"Daughter, you have a heart of kindness and a head for truth. Who does not need a friend of that kind? And he will have need of it now more than ever before. Shrink not from it."

73

She nodded her head, taking his words very seriously to heart. And he added, "'One stands and another holds him up, and the glory of both is in each.' Someone or other wrote that down once, I believe."

Her face beamed a knowing smile and she replied, "I have read it well, sir—words of a certain old man I know. Very wise he is."

His eyes twinkled, "Indeed? Well, one learns a few things over time. Child, you are delightfully well-read for a Winn."

They turned to enter the room as she whispered a confession, "It comes of an Ahlrik mother."

The Elders took their usual places at the table. Nora seated herself next to Phlycia, with Fen sitting next to her and Aegius across from him. Sabian took up the place at the end of the table; and with these nine present, the council began.

Kholrihk addressed everyone first. "The business of the morning is this: Ahmahnric is on the rise again. Here in Kysmarc we are hearing dark rumors of alliances with Eastern Barbarians. There are concerning reports of new fire raids coming from Ahlred," he looked to Phlycia, who nodded affirmingly. "And most troublesome news from Dresdor," he turned to Huros, who now spoke to the group.

"A strange folk have been migrating to Dresdor over the last some years. In small number initially, in larger number these days. They were of no account to anyone at first, but at present if you consider the positions of influence within Dresden society, you will find they have carved quite a place for themselves. Numerous roles of leadership—administrators, advisors, Parliament members—always held by the Dresden have landed in the hands of these outsiders."

Aegius broke in asking, "Who are they?"

"They call themselves the Norians and claim to come from a clan in some far-lying land to the northeast in the Outer Regions—Nor Que Pneuris it is known in their tongue. Many in Dresdor have been very pleased with these Norians, for in appearances they seem to move very well along with the common ideals of the people, namely that Dresdor is destined to rise to greatness. The old talk is beginning again, with the Norians pushing it most strongly—that Dresdor should take its place over the other tribes at last."

Xophnius huffed scornfully, and Bryn sighed a long, tired sigh. Expressions of question and concern were worn by many around the table. Huros continued, "But not everyone has been drawn in by the Norian rhetoric. Some of the Dresden have doubted the motive and true aim of these outsiders. Granted they are fewer than those who support them, but they are there. For now, at least. The gentleman who has accompanied me here is one of such thought. He is of the Dresbane, one of the highest ranking families in Dresdor." Huros gave a nod in Sabian's direction, and the man stood nobly from his seat and addressed the council.

"Madams and Sirs, you have been most gracious in allowing my presence before so great a company. And I extend my thanks for the opportunity to discuss the case of these concerning times for Dresdor."

Before he could continue, Fen raised his voice, "My apologies, may I ask a question before we proceed?"

With the table's attention he said, "I do not understand why Kholrihk spoke in the beginning that our business was with Ahmahnric and yet the trouble seems to be a group of immigrants in Dresdor. Why should one have to do with the other?"

Bryn answered plainly, "I can say this: you will not find one of the five here who believes the trouble in

Dresdor begins with the Norians. No. It begins with Ahmahnric as surely as you sit in that chair."

"That is our thinking, madam," said Sabian. "The Norians claim that they stand for Dresdor, and many believe them. But there are some—myself at the very front—who believe in reality they are pawns of Ahmahnric, who likely stand to gain something when they have handed him Dresdor."

"Or handed him the entire kingdom," said Phlycia.

"Kingdom?!" asked Nora, aghast.

"It is not unlikely," Kholrihk said. "Ahmahnric set his heart on ruling the Four Corners a long time ago."

Xophnius nodded. "And we have seen his work on many fronts to weaken the tribes. He has sown fear, division, and chaos throughout. How much longer before they are easy prey for this monster he is creating out of Dresdor?"

Xophnius had his eyes locked on Fen as he spoke, and the latter was clearly unsure how much of it all he believed. But he listened. Intently he listened.

"You doubt, friend?" asked Sabian, looking at Fen.

"I remain cautious of believing that every ill stroke comes from the hand of an ancient foe," Fen replied.

Nora lowered her eyes, not wanting to see the Elders' reactions to her friend's words.

"Well, Xophnius," said Bryn, "you have your work."

The look on Xophnius's face suggested that he rather agreed with the woman, and it was Aegius who answered Fen—and answered him well, "You do not know what you have not seen, brother, and you cannot be faulted for that. But do not despise the wisdom of those who have seen, and who share it in order that you might know."

Kholrihk followed with the announcement that the Elders had decided to assemble a group of men and women from all the Four Corners of the Earth—a

Resistance—against Ahmahnric and his growing force among the tribes.

"I confess, sir," said Sabian excitedly, "that such a thing was my very hope. The time is already late if we are to uncover and overcome his purposes. I have thus far gathered a band of thirty loyal men who are ready at my call for this mission. If we can unveil whatever foul scheme is being wrought by Ahmahnric and the Norians, the hearts of the men of Dresdor far and wide will rise up with us. But I came here to seek first alliance with the Elders, for I know we cannot stand against Ahmahnric without you."

It was quiet around the table for an awkward moment. Then Kholrihk spoke. "Excellent, Sabian. With your passion and vision you bring gifts that are sorely needed and will no doubt prove invaluable to the movement. The Elders are appointing Fen of Winderlawk as the Command of the Resistance—"

"Me?!" Fen blurted out in a shocked voice that stopped the man abruptly. Truthfully the look of astonishment on Sabian's face was no less than that on Fen's own. "Why in the Four Corners would you choose me?"

He looked around the table at a complete loss. He noticed that Sabian had fixed questioning—almost frantic—eyes on Huros, as if wanting him to speak into this most unexpected (and clearly unsatisfactory) decision.

Xophnius answered, "It is a surprising turn of the course for everyone, but its merit flows deep from the discernment of this council. We will forego argument for the defense of our actions and let time prove us wise."

"Let time prove you wise?" asked Sabian. "I'm sorry but if you are proved wrong it will be with the lives of the men and women of Dresdor... and of the rest of the Four Corners for that matter. Huros?"

But the man interrupted him with a firm tone, "Pax, Sabian. This is the way forward."

Sabian still stood, mouth half open, at an utter loss. Nora and Aegius, hawk-like, watched Fen. And Fen had locked eyes with Xophnius, as if he might read the man's mind if only he tried hard enough. For a moment no one seemed to know what to say. And then Fen gathered himself together with a deep breath, "Why not the Elders? You know far more than us Ahmahnric's ways. Why this Resistance?"

"It is not the business of the Elders to fight Ahmahnric," answered Xophnius. "The work of the Elders has always been restoring Kembarius's heir to the throne."

Bryn continued, "We have taken the matter of fighting Ahmahnric into hand more than once since his rebellion. You may know how it went if you read the Battles of Bolkahn and Longris, or of the Uprising at Saldawn. It is not the Elders who will defeat Ahmahnric. It is the heir of Kembarius."

"Nevertheless," said Xophnius, "he must be pushed back, for his power threatens the Four Corners more every day."

"And what do you think I can accomplish that five Elders cannot?" asked Fen, incredulous.

"You speak as though you were alone," said Aegius. "We four ride with you, brother, and the Dresden has said there are thirty more at the ready. There will be hundreds if not thousands who will rise to the cause."

"A moment," interjected Sabian strongly, "the faithful of my kin are... looking to *me*... to lead Dresdor. I cannot promise to deliver three men who will follow a..." He held his tongue as he looked helplessly at Fen.

Nora finished his sentence coolly, "a Winn? Is it so inconceivable that strength might come from anywhere but Dresdor, sir?"

Fen put his hand on her arm, a suggestion that she refrain from such remarks, but she answered that suggestion aloud, "It is plain he meant it. They cannot be expected to follow a man from Winderlawk, can they Mr. Dresbane?"

Sabian did not answer her that moment, and she pressed him further, "Can *you*?"

"Can I?" he repeated as if he did not know what she meant by it.

"Yes, can you follow a man from Winderlawk?" she asked pointedly, and all at the table curiously awaited his response. It did not come, for truly it was a crushing moment for Sabian Dresbane and he did not know how exactly he would come through it. He sat down in his chair sullenly and lowered his eyes to his fists that lay clenched on the table.

It was surprisingly Fen who spoke up for him. "The reservations of our friend here are not ungrounded. You have not stated why you should think me the leader of this force. You say 'Resistance' but let us speak plainly— you mean there is a war to come. Against an enemy I have never seen," he paused and thought a moment before continuing. "Perhaps things are exactly as you suspect, and the enemy against us is none other than Ahmahnric himself. I am no soldier. What can I know of how to defeat him? And forgive the impudence, but what can possibly be your reasoning for choosing me?"

Fen looked intuitively to Xophnius for the answer to his question, as did everyone else present, and Xophnius weighed his response carefully.

"Our reasons are not for everyone to know at present, however disagreeable that may seem," he said. And turning to Fen he added, "I ask for your trust in this, a steep appeal to be certain. And sir," he addressed

Sabian directly now, "if you fear the Dresden will not follow a Winn, what would you say to the objection that a Dresden—such as yourself—would be followed not by Winn, nor by Ahlrik, nor by Kysmen?"

With resolute spirit and a fire in his voice Sabian answered, "I say I would find a way. I would give them reason to follow."

Kholrihk seemed pleased with this response, "Well done then, you have solved your own dilemma."

The Elders all nodded in agreement, but the others seemed confused.

"What do you mean, sir?" asked Sabian.

Phlycia replied gently, "If you could inspire three tribes to follow the other, could you not inspire one tribe to do the same?"

A smile escaped Nora's lips, which she tried to hide quickly with a more serious expression as poor Sabian resigned himself to the situation.

"I will do what I can," he replied weakly.

"Well then," said Xophnius, "the one who came to lead is willing to follow." He looked at Fen, as did all at the table, when he said next, "What remains to be seen is whether the one who came to follow is willing to lead?"

9

A BITTER WIND BLOWS

Wake up. Something inside him was urging him out of sleep. It was dark and cool when Fen opened his eyes. The hard ground was damp beneath him, and his body was tired and stiff. The stars of the early morning hours shone against the dark blue canvas above. Mellow tones of an owl called softly from a tree somewhere up the hill from the valley where they camped. Blinking his eyes, he sat up feeling very disoriented and relieved to be awake; what bizarre and unsettling dreams. He exhaled deeply and rubbed his hands over his face. And then he saw him—the Dresden with short curly hair sleeping on a patch of nearby grass. Xophnius was laid out just to his right, with Khaz over on the left. And seeing the present company surrounding him, he realized nothing of it had been a dream at all.

He had travelled to Kysmarc an orphaned farm-hand who knew very little of the world beyond Winderlawk. Now he was returning, just days later, at the command of a Resistance force given the fairly unbelievable mission of unifying the Four Corners to stand against Ahmahnric. Who would have ever expected such a baffling scenario? And what exactly was he supposed to do about all this anyway? And a hundred other questions pounded his brain with no respect for the unreasonably early hour of the day at which he found himself awake.

Aegius lay closest to Fen, just a few feet away. He was asleep on his back, knife in hand at his side, an observation that Fen found strangely reassuring. *Well, if I don't know what in the Four Corners I'm doing, at least I've got Aegius to help me*, he thought to himself. And deciding that there was no real likelihood of any more sleep being had, he got to his feet and decided to walk and think and hopefully clear his head. That he felt this overwhelmed before the sun had even shown its face did not bode well for the day.

Fen made his way carefully to the edge of the camp and noticed, for the first time, Liam perched on a boulder that sat between the open valley beyond and the sleeping travelers with the hill rising immediately behind them. He approached the rock quietly and paused before the vigilant man.

"Have you kept watch all night, Liam?" With his eyes growing more and more accustomed to the dark, Fen could make out the sharp features of Liam's face, a face which gave the impression of belonging to someone quite older than Fen even though the two were about the same in years.

"It's been easy work this night," Liam replied.

"Even so," said Fen, "the ride will be long today. Go sleep; there is yet a few hours before the sun rises. I'll take your place here."

Liam shook his head with a pleasant but definitive manner, saying, "I don't believe so, Commander, but I appreciate your offer."

The term "Commander" struck Fen something like the feeling one has when the wind has been knocked out of him, and he knows the next breath will come and yet feels it may not come soon enough. That was the sort of earnest and sober feeling that settled somewhere in his stomach at the moment. He tried to shake it off and told Liam, "Still, everyone needs sleep."

But Liam was not to be moved in the slightest. "I am

the Watch, sir. You have your role, and I have mine."

It was the moment Fen knew everything had changed and would never be the same. Strange that it should be so, he felt—that he should have sat in the council with the Elders of the Four Corners of the Earth and be named the Commander of the Resistance and yet somehow feel it more deeply when a young Winn should believe it enough to sit on a rock all night and keep watch.

Fen nodded his acceptance of the situation and walked on, heading for the stream that entered the valley nearby. He walked to warm and stretch his stiff body, but he walked more so to gain command of his thoughts and emotions before he should dare to command anything or anyone else. The ground crunched softly underfoot, and the melodic sound of the rippling stream grew nearer as he moved steadily through the tall grasses. Oddly, the more he tried to prepare himself for the future, it was memories of the past that came rushing to his mind.

He was maybe five, hiding in the loft of the stable at the farm. Grable's voice was calling for him, but he buried himself all the more in that sweet smelling straw with his tear streaked face and his angry fists. Grable stood long at the doorway asking in his easy farmerly way who it was up in that loft. Finally, Fen told him exactly who it was: *nobody* was up there. Very clear about that had the children of Ainsworth been. He was *nobody*... no father, no mother, no business pretending to be a Winn.

"Let's see about that now." That was what Grable said, and he simply turned and left. Returning a few minutes later, he called for nobody to join him; and Fen did because, though he was heartbroken, he was not disobedient. And also because he was only five, and the resolve of one at this age to live alone for the rest of his life is really not likely to thrive much beyond the realm of about twelve minutes.

Grable's hand covered in dirt and sweat grasped the boy's bathed in dirt and tears, and he took him out into the daylight. From his pocket Grable retrieved a single seed in its hard shell and lay it in his own worn, leathery palm.

Did Fen know where he got that seed? The boy shook his head. Had Fen seen the tree that produced that seed? Again the boy shook his head. Did Fen suspect that nothing would grow from that seed if he had not seen the seed's ancestors? Fen sniffed back his stubborn tears and shrugged his shoulders.

"Maybe it will be the biggest tree south of the Lawksbur. Let's find out, you and me." Grable said those words bent down with his strong and tender face right in front of the boy's, and Fen felt for just that second that perhaps he would grow up and be the greatest man who ever lived.

The two of them chose a special patch of ground for that seed near a bench that had been Mrs. Lawk's treasured spot for watching the sunrise (one of the precious few memories of her that Grable had shared like that). And though it had been nearly sixteen years now since the farmer had found nobody crying in a stable loft, many were the times still when Fen would make his way for that bench so that he might look at his tree which had grown impressively tall and strong over those years. Thinking of it somehow settled him even now.

The morning was startling to bustle with the sounds of all things waking, and the sun was beginning to cast its warm light across the valley as Fen made his way back to the camp. Everyone was up and about, readying themselves and their horses for the day's ride when Fen arrived.

"Where have you been?" asked Nora, her fingers

rapidly twisting her hair into a long braid as she spoke.

"Just a walk," he answered.

"I wonder that you should go off like that here," she said with a bit of uncertainty. "We are not so far from where those men attacked us."

With a glance over his shoulder Fen replied, "I believe I was covered."

A few moments later in fact Liam appeared, nodded to Fen and Nora and kept walking straight towards Aegius who was saddling his steed. They exchanged a few private words, after which Aegius nodded his head in a manner of approval. He turned his attention back to the gentle, white horse in front of him, while Liam found himself face to face with Sabian.

"Look here," Sabian began in a rather authoritative sort of way, "I heard you discussing our route to Winderlawk, and I think I have something to say about it."

Liam reached for his saddle pack that lay near his feet and pulled out an apple. After taking a bite, he replied to Sabian with a simple, "How so?"

"I heard you tell Xophnius that we were best to keep the middle road all the way back," Sabian said, "but you yourselves know very well the danger of raiding parties that may be faced on this way. As I understand, it is only a few hours more to the journey if we cut south and meet with the road that crosses the River Marcs at Kerr."

Liam shook his head, nearly half the apple already devoured. He took another juicy bite and said, "You cannot cross there this time of spring. The river will be too high."

"But how can you be so certain?" Sabian asked with a doubting air.

"If the raiders are what you fear, sir, I can have Wylla ride at your side," Liam answered with thick disdain in his voice.

Aegius turned in a flash before Sabian could get an angry word out, "Liam." His voice was iron and his eyes penetrating. "It is neither fear nor foolishness to avoid a raid if it be possible." Then he turned to Sabian with an acknowledging look, "It cannot be helped; there is no crossing at Kerr this season. We will trust that we have bow and sword plenty enough to meet whatever we may."

Fen watched Sabian sulk off and observed the reprimanding look Liam received from Aegius, as well as the slight shrug he gave in return. It was not the closest band of comrades that rode off westward later that hour.

The party had ridden with very little conversation for several hours as the sun rose to its towering place in the bright sky. They were nearing the boundary of the river, coming now once again to the Valley of Shaw. Nora's heart beat a little quicker remembering the furious race across this turf. She rode next to Wylla in their procession of twos—Xophnius and Fen at the lead, Sabian and Aegius next, the women behind them and Liam and Khaz at the rear.

The valley stretched before them the epitome of tranquility today, and the horses went along at an easy pace. Fen's voice broke the silence as he glanced over to Xophnius.

"The raiders we met here... do you know who they were?"

"I do not precisely know who they were, but their horses and arms were from the north," Xophnius answered. "Did you notice their blades?"

"I did," said Fen. "I've never seen a sword of such metal before."

"Indeed. It is nyloth, and it is particular to the far Northern Plains of the Outer Regions where it is mined.

It is heavier than one might wish for a blade but formidable to be sure. Ahmahnric's warriors have long used such weaponry, though I have never seen it wielded this far south before," explained Xophnius.

"Do you think it was Ahmahnric's men who gave chase to you then?" asked Sabian from behind.

"It is quite possible," replied Xophnius, "though unlikely they were lying in wait deliberately for us. I should think if he knew of our journey and meant to stop us, we would have faced a considerably larger foe."

"If they were his men from the north, what are they doing down here?" asked Fen.

"I think the Commander of the Resistance is asking the right question. Now you have only to find the answer to it," Xophnius replied with a smile to Fen.

"Well," said Fen dryly, "and find a way to stop him from undoing the Four Corners of the Earth by uniting a group of people who want nothing to do with each other."

"Well, yes," replied Xophnius, "there is also that."

As they entered the open countryside of Winderlawk, the low, rolling hills reached out under a wide blue sky as far as the eye could see, with only a few groves of poplars here or there rising up from the sea of grassy green. The group fell to discussing a number of issues, as they drew ever nearer their destination.

It had been decided that they would make the Lawk farm a sort of base for the company until a more suitable location could be procured. You will no doubt have suspected that Sabian was none too pleased about heading to Winderlawk instead of straight to Dresdor. But Xophnius had made the argument that they must have a place where they would be less visible, where they could come and go without fear that one of Ahmahnric's spies was behind them at every turn. And with Fen and most of the present company hailing from the quiet lands of Winderlawk, it only made sense that they should start from there.

But late the next morning when they were reaching the end of their expedition, they discovered, to their surprise, that things in "quiet Winderlawk" were anything but quiet. They were on the road (the same dirt road in fact that Fen and Nora had been walking when the mastids struck), and they heard before they saw. There was an angry racket, a mob-like chaos of yells and shouts sounding from the swamp ahead.

Fen and Xophnius urged speed from their mounts. The others followed suit and so came speedily to the edge of the Lawksbur at the ferry crossing where the following scene was unfolding.

Sixty or so men had formed a line along the water's edge where the ferry was moored. These happened to all be Winn of northern Winderlawk. Arms locked together, they stood like a human barricade facing an equal number of men who wailed against them with cries of rage and fists to the sky. This group happened to be entirely Winn from the south. In the murky water behind the defensive line, a sort of wooden barge had been set afire. It sent up a thick smoke that got caught in the dense trees and made the air sharp and biting. It was difficult to distinguish the exact words and accusations and threats that were being launched by each side to the other.

Fen motioned to Nora and Liam to stay at the rear of the scene. He sent Wylla and Khaz to the left, Aegius and Sabian around the right, and he rode—himself and Xophnius—right through the very middle of the heated throng with his right arm raised high and a few shouts to the men on the ground below him, "Hold! Hold!"

The unexpected sight of a band of men on horseback

riding into the middle of things was enough to silence several of the men, but others raged on wholly undeterred. Fen and Xophnius were now exactly between the line of northerners on the one side and the angry mob on the other, and Fen called for them all to stand down, but his voice was drowned in the din of their shouts.

"Xophnius," Fen had to almost yell to be heard by the man just next to him. Xophnius responded with a sweep of his arm to the sheath at his back and drew his blade. This changed the tone of the gathering entirely the very moment it happened, for although the men were clearly furious, they were at least unarmed.

"Pax, friends!" Fen called out over the crowd that was now considerably quieter, having given their attention to the man with steel. "What is this?"

A roar began to swell immediately as a multitude answered back, but Fen held up both his hands and shouted again, "Hold, men! Hold!" And the shouting died down again.

"Denmoure!" Fen shouted to one man close at hand whom he recognized from Ainsworth. "What is going on?"

"We've had enough! That's what!" he shouted back angrily, and his side of the mob cheered in hearty agreement.

Another man beside Denmoure cried out, "They don't know what it's like! Never lost a blade of grass to those mastids, they've not!" Again, cries and echoes of approval.

"Pax!" Fen repeated in a commanding voice.

"He doesn't know!" said a tall fellow named Tullian, whose land bordered the Lawk farm to the west. He spoke to the crowd, "He's been gone!"

"Tell him, Tullian!" yelled Denmoure, among others.

Tullian spoke loudly, and the group grew very nearly

silent that he might be heard. "Two days ago, Fen. Mastids came. No storm. No warning. They just came. Eslow here lost every last lamb born this season. The Burk place next to him near lost an entire crop of beans. And your man," Tullian paused here for a moment. "Your man's not been conscious since yesterday morning... caught it bad trying to save the Hollowsman boy who was out playing when they struck."

At the news of Grable, Fen shot a sharp, anxious look to Aegius, who responded with a knowing nod. He pulled his horse away from the crowd and galloped off in the direction of the Lawk farm. Nora had immediately done the same at the mention of the man's name.

Fen tried to focus his attention on the present situation. "So why the problem with our friends from the north?"

"All we want is security, same as they have!" Denmoure shouted.

"That's right!" a mass of voices echoed.

The northern Winn who stood closest to Fen's right, a solid bear of a man named Thasperus, spoke up for his side, "You can't just be thinking to bring your animals and your families and your lives north of the Lawksbur! It's madness!" And the line of men finally had their chance to voice their approval.

Fen questioned Thasperus, "What do you mean?"

"I mean they said plain enough they're moving north—a whole slew of them! They don't have land up there. It's not their place!"

"Well enough for you, Thasperus!" shouted Tullian. "You never lost a thing like these people!"

The crowd was getting out of hand once more on both sides, but Liam sent an arrow whizzing overhead into a towering cypress tree. The mob quieted.

"Do you mean to move north?" Fen asked Tullian.

"Some do," he replied. "It's not safe anymore, Fen. There's men want to move their families where they can look out for them, and I ask: who can blame them?"

Fen scanned the faces of the men gathered around him. He saw fear, anger, uncertainty. And when he spoke, it was with the voice of a Commander. "Listen, friends, there is trouble to be sure. But let us not abandon homes yet. It is a bitter wind that blows, but better to push it back than bow to its wishes."

"Meaning what, Fen?" Tullian asked what many were thinking.

"Meaning I'm heading out for the Southern Caves in the morning, and any man who wants to ride with me is welcome," said Fen.

There was not a single voice to be heard among them. For one thing, the Southern Caves were considered, at best, the most dangerous and wildest place within a hundred miles of Winderlawk. At worst, some believed them a haunted place of all things evil and dark. They were, after all, the breeding grounds of the mastids. Who could be sure what else lurked there?

It was very few who had ever gone so far as those desolate caverns. In truth, it had been six or seven years since anyone had ventured past southern Winderlawk to the Caves which marked the border with the deserts of the Outer Regions beyond. And that party had not returned. So you may imagine that there was not a wild rush of volunteers to ride out with the young man in the morning.

Finally, a man spoke. "And what will you do at the Caves?"

"Come and see for yourself," Fen answered.

10

TO THE CAVES

The situation at the Lawk farm was as serious as Fen had feared. He and the others had reached there after leaving the swamp to find Grable in bed, his skin a sickly greenish color and damp with a sour sweat. Over his fitfully sleeping body stood Nora's mother. She had been doing her best to care for the man since the attack, but it had not gone well and she bore the distress of it clearly on her tired face.

She had sent Aegius back to the swamp to collect more leaves of the himbus plant, and Nora worked over a boiling pot in the kitchen at her mother's instruction. Xophnius examined the man closely, and Emaliys (for so was the name of Nora's mother) watched intently and answered his many questions as carefully as she could. Fen simply sat at Grable's side, holding the man's hand in his own.

"Did you drain this wound on his left shoulder?" asked Xophnius, inspecting a festering fang puncture.

"Twice," Emaliys answered. "But you can see the infection spreading still. I do not understand."

"Indeed," Xophnius said gravely, studying a series of bite marks down the man's arm.

Emaliys smoothed back a few strands of her reddish brown hair that had come loose, and sighed wearily. "It's much worse than I've seen before."

"You have certainly done what you could, madam," said Xophnius kindly, "but there are some things I have at my place if he is to pull through. And even with them..." His voice trailed off, and he looked at Fen with a sympathy that gave the young man a knot in the pit of his stomach. "I will return within the hour," he added, and nodding to Nora and the pot she was stirring said, "See if you can manage a bit of that brew down the poor man."

Fen spent the rest of the day at Grable's side, with Xophnius instructing Emaliys in various methods of treating the injuries. Nora went here and there as the two needed clean rags or boiled water or more root grated into powder. Everyone else remained outside the house, saying very little and perhaps wondering how they would fare the next day storming the castle, so to speak, of the creatures that had produced such grim results in the man who lay inside.

It was late when Fen whispered something into Grable's ear, finally rose to his feet, and went outside for a breath of night air. Nora followed him out onto the wooden steps, wanting so much to say something helpful and feeling that was hopelessly impossible.

"I'm so sorry," she finally said.

Fen just nodded, then replied, "Your mother is an angel."

"She is," Nora agreed. "Will we still leave in the morning?"

"It depends on who you mean by 'we'," Fen answered.

Nora stiffened a bit. "You know very well what I mean."

The moon was full and bright, so that it was quite easy for each to read the expression on the face of the other. It was clear they shared a difference of opinion and that they were preparing to deal with that difference.

"Nora, you are not going tomorrow," Fen said quite matter-of-factly.

"Well, maybe you suppose I don't mind being left out of things entirely," she said rather sarcastically, "but I believe I *will* go with everyone tomorrow. I don't see you forbidding anyone else." Rot, why did her temper always speak before her better judgment? She knew full well that telling him what she would do against his wishes was the last way to change his mind, but even so, she could not bring herself to back down.

"You'll not go tomorrow—," he started, but she interrupted.

"Wylla is going! I saw her packing up. So if you think because I am a girl that I can't—"

But Fen was not about to be moved and said plainly, "Wylla is a better shot from a mount at full gallop than most men from their post on a wall."

She found this response immensely irritating, but before she could reply he spoke again... and this time in a gentler tone. "*Please stay.* Your mother will need help with Grable."

This quieted Nora considerably, and she found herself nodding before she quite knew she'd given in. And then she said in a soft voice, "Of course. Of course I'll help look after him."

It was dawn when the seven rode out, heading first north, back to the swamp. Eleven of the mob men had agreed to go; Fen hoped perhaps six of them actually would. It was three they found waiting for them when they arrived at the Lawksbur: Tullian, Eslow, and— surprisingly— Thasperus.

"Not quite the full number is it?" Sabian remarked indignantly.

94

"You've not seen the mastids," Khaz answered back.

Fen greeted the three, "Thank you for coming."

"Yes, well," muttered Thasperus, "let's get on with it."

"But first, one thing," said Fen.

The party that soon headed south from the swamp that morning was quite something to see. For Fen had required that they all bathe in the swampish muck on the chance that it might provide some protection for them when they reached the Caves. Xophnius and Aegius had thought it an excellent idea and were quick to wade into the murk and submerge themselves without reservation. Liam, Khaz, and Wylla had followed fairly obediently. Tullian and Eslow were more reluctant but finally agreed to the distasteful task. Sabian and Thasperus, however, swore on all manner of holy things that they would never so much as set a bootstrap in that filth.

Perhaps you are familiar with the truth that when one uses enormous words such as "never," he should expect the universe to begin the undoing of such speech almost immediately. Such was the case for the two men who would "never" set foot in the swamp, for it was no more than five minutes before Sabian was covered head to foot—and in a most surprising manner.

You may imagine his disdain, sitting astride his horse in his fine Dresden wear and watching his comrades rise, soaked in the mire and murk of the swamp. But now imagine his horror as Xophnius gave a peculiar long, low whistle at which Sabian's horse began walking towards the man who gave it (who happened to still be in the swamp). Sabian pulled at the reins, but the horse remarkably went on undaunted towards the aged man who held out his hand to the beast. Sabian yelled and howled and called down curses that were quite a long way from making any sense whatsoever, but the horse was wading deeper and deeper, until only its neck and head remained in the air above, and Sabian was finally forced to dismount and pull at the beast in the direction of the shore. The laughing and taunting was kept to a respectable minimum; and when all was said and done, Sabian (and his horse no less) had indeed been baptized in the Lawksbur.

From there it was a short matter of explaining to Thasperus that he would no doubt make the very first target for the mastids, being the only one who had refused the swamp's mysterious benefits; and they hoped he had put his affairs in order and other such well wishes.

And so it was that the last man found his resolve after all for obeying Fen's mandate, and thus ten filthy persons began the expedition south. It was around 7 A.M. at the time, which meant they could expect to reach the caves by late morning—possibly as early as 10:00 if they kept a good pace.

The Southern Caves truly were the last place any sane person in Winderlawk would want to go. It was an arid place of large rocky formations, bits of scrubby bushes and a few desert-dwelling ramerham trees jutting up here and there. Beyond this place stretched the beginning of the Great Sand Deserts of the Outer Regions. A few small outposts laid scattered to the east and west of the Caves, populated mostly by unsavory characters who belonged to nowhere and to no one.

As for the Caves themselves, not so very much was known about them at this time, being as it was that so few Winn had ever ventured near them. It was generally thought that there was a vast underground cavernous system with several entry points from the ground above. That is to say, we should more properly think of one massive cave with multiple entrances rather than a series of several and separate caves. And in this theory, the

Winn were to be proved correct.

Having reached the Caves exactly as hoped, the company set about the plan that Fen had laid out for them during the previous few hours. They worked in absolute silence, in fervent hopes that they would not disturb the mastids, bringing on an attack. For although many details of the plan had been worked out and accounted for, it seemed, unhappily, that this particular risk must be left to time and chance.

They worked in pairs, beginning on horseback. Fen and Aegius rode together. Xophnius went with Sabian, and so forth. Parting ways, each pair rode throughout the area and surveyed the landscape in search of cave entrances. In this work they had a fortunate aid. Being as barren as it was, there was not so very much vegetation to be seen across the land. The main exception to this was the Bristle Weed, a plant that happens to thrive in the area due to the specific fertilizing effect of mastid dung. Its wiry stalks with their grey, whiskery leaves grow taller than most men, making it quite visible on the landscape; and the plants are found most plentifully in close proximity to the cave mouths themselves where the mastidal fertilizer is frequently deposited.

Fen and Aegius had gone westward when the hunting party separated ways, and in less than fifteen minutes they had spotted their first cave mouth. They dismounted at a good distance and crept with the lightest steps possible towards the gaping black hole. It was of a fair size, being about one horse length in both height and width. They fell to the work at hand with as much speed as could be managed under the restraints of careful silence.

Fen pulled from his belt a leather pouch and poured a small mound of purplish powder into his gloved hand. Then with a sweeping motion he emptied his palm, sprinkling the powder into the dark unknown. Aegius lifted one of the large rocks near his feet and placed it at the mouth of the cave. Fen laid another next to it. And working like this with the surrounding stones and occasional logs or branches from the sparse trees, they had effectively shut up the opening entirely in about forty minutes.

They returned to their horses, much sweatier than before and much smellier as well; for the swamp odors were intensifying brilliantly as the men worked in the heat, so that they could hardly bare their own stench. But when they had spotted a patch of Bristle Weed around another cave entrance ten minutes further west, they quietly dismounted and immediately set to it again. This one was quite small and was blocked in no more than the time it had taken to find it. And they went on like so, till the sun was high in the sky and the sweat mixed with swamp mire ran in their eyes and stung fiercely. And the odious smell was so unbearable that it gagged them at times.

The worst of the afternoon heat had passed when most of the party had returned to their meeting point. Liam and Wylla were absent yet, but everyone else had made it back having emptied most of the leather pouches carried by all and having blockaded every entry point possible as far as they could tell. One opening more remained, and this was the primary entrance. It was substantially larger than all the others and seemed it would be the most difficult part of the affair, for they had been wholly unsure whether they would be able to shut it up or not.

Now observing it just a few hundred horse-lengths to the east of them, they felt it might be possible to close off perhaps half of it at the most, which presented a serious problem. The plan had been this: the powder which they had been distributing at the cave mouths was a poison Xophnius had acquired on one of his journeys in the Outer Regions. Extremely flammable, it produced an explosive and toxic gas when lit. Their desire was obviously to isolate the mastids in the caves and then kill them with the poisonous fumes, and it was hard to see how this was possible if the mastids had a way of escape.

"There was a large deposit of crumbled rock and stone a ten minute's ride south," offered Sabian. "We could haul it in."

"It would take half a day to bring in enough material to block that hole," replied Aegius. "And we do not know if we have five minutes more. What if they swarm at sundown?"

"We could build a fire in front of the cave..." shrugged Eslow, "keep them from coming out that way."

But Xophnius assured him that the last thing one wanted to do was to build a bonfire where there was kahgstiyl to be ignited. It was one thing, he had said, to sneak in a bit of lit kindling from behind a wall of rock; it was quite another to set a raging fire in the open with the volatile powder in such proximity.

Most of the group seemed to grow rather discouraged at this point. They were hot and filthy, tired and ravenous. And it seemed now that they had come to the brink of it and there was no way forward. Thasperus rubbed his dirty brow, frustrated. "Well, what's to be done then? Or else all this mess was for nothing."

"Eslow," began Fen with a hopeful note, "I believe you have the idea. But we need Liam and Wylla." He looked around quickly, obviously formulating some scheme in his head and eager to move forward. "Where are they?"

Xophnius stared at him, "You were listening, were you not? You heard me say that you cannot light a fire at the mouth of that cave. It is impossible."

"Yes, I know," Fen said eagerly. "The fire—how far back must it be? Mark it for me. Where are those two?" He strained his eyes across the distance, hoping for signs of them.

"I am sure they will be here soon," replied Aegius. "What is your thought?"

Fen relayed his theory quickly, and Xophnius felt it was indeed possible, assuming the two returned and all four bowmen were able to work quickly.

"We will build the fire now and trust they will be here when we need them," said Fen.

So Eslow, Tullian, and Thasperus set about building the fire on Xophnius's mark—about fifty horse-lengths from the entrance of the cave, while Aegius and Khaz busied themselves preparing their arsenal. Xophnius approached Sabian and Fen and held up a full pouch of kahgstiyl.

"It will need to be distributed evenly from wall to wall, at least ten horse-lengths inside the cave," he said soberly.

Sabian stood frozen in his boots, eyeing the sack of powder with a slight and fretful twitch. *Ten horse-lengths inside the cave?* he thought. Nobody had said anything about going *inside*. But the next moment Fen had snatched the leather sack from the man's hand and started in the direction of the cave.

It caught Aegius's attention, and he turned quickly to see Fen leaving. "No!" he called out sharply, surprising everyone— most of all Fen. "Give it to me," Aegius said, "I will take it. And be back in time to fire." He walked after Fen, who had halted.

"I am able," Fen responded. But Aegius reached him in the next step and held out his hand for the pouch.

"Indeed, brother. Ability is not the matter." His hand

waited for the sack.

Fen paused, feeling the heaviness of such a moment, where one man so freely holds out his life in the place of yours. Then gently Fen placed the bag in the hand before him, "Elethas keep you."

Aegius set out with a strong stride towards the cave, and Fen turned to the others. "Start the fire," he told Tullian. And to Xophnius he asked, "If the others are not back will the two be enough?"

"I do not know," Xophnius answered. "I think it unlikely. But I do not know."

Khaz feverishly finished his work while he stole frequent glances over his shoulder at his brother who approached the mouth of the cave. Moments later Aegius disappeared into the black. They all watched now with anxiousness and admiration. A small flame had begun to burn in the spot they had chosen for it. Khaz had nocked an arrow onto his bowstring and stood over the fire with keen eyes set on the entrance to the mastid hole.

Fen watched expectantly, wondering how a few seconds could seem so intolerably long and wondering why his friend had not yet reappeared. It had been time enough now, hadn't it? Yes, he felt certain.

"What's gone wrong?" he asked Xophnius. "He is too long inside."

"Perhaps," Xophnius said with a worried tone as well. "Give him a moment."

It was several things that all happened next. First, there was the sound of thundering hoof beats. Liam and Wylla were approaching at a gallop from the east. Second, there was a distant echo of shrieks that began swelling from the cave. Then Aegius appeared, charging out of the black and yelling with everything in him, "Fire! They're coming! Fire!"

Khaz dipped an arrow that had been wrapped and

prepared into the fire, and it caught blaze quickly. He looked at Xophnius.

"Do not fire! He is too close!" Xophnius said quickly.

"And if they make it out then we are too late!" said Sabian. He grabbed the bow Aegius had left and in a moment had another flaming arrow directed towards the cave. Aegius was yelling for them to fire as he ran, and Xophnius was commanding them to wait. Liam and Wylla were almost there, and now it was seen that there were riders in brown hoods with black swords pursuing them some distance back.

Sabian and Khaz held ready. Aegius was half the distance across the field. Xophnius counted their shot, "Five! Four! Three!"

Liam and Wylla fairly leapt from their saddles. Following Fen's quick command, they fit arrows to their strings. In the next breath at Xophnius's word, they let loose their flames with Khaz and Sabian, then immediately four more arrows went into the fire and were shot into the target. A third set was fired by the time Aegius reached the group. He turned just in time to see the greatest surge of the explosion, which brought the entire mouth of the cave crumbling down in rock and rubble.

The mastid shrieks ceased almost instantly. But there was not a moment to breathe yet.

"There are eight," started Liam, still trying to catch his breath. "We stumbled upon them to the east."

They all turned to find indeed eight riders charging towards them at full speed, weapons raised.

11

A BROTHERHOOD BOUGHT

In a single, furious minute our company had mounted their horses and drawn their weapons, preparing to meet the oncoming attack. But there was no attack, or rather one should say there was no attack at that time. For when the hooded riders realized they were no longer pursuing two horsemen but instead were now facing a number greater than their own, they gave up their chase and turned swiftly back the way they came.

"Do we go after them?" pressed Wylla.

"They are not warriors who flee," said Aegius, "which makes me think it wasteful to track them. But I will do as you say." He looked at Fen, who knew the decision must be an immediate one.

"I agree they are no warriors, and yet they are troublesome all the same. Had we not met their kind at Shaw as well, perhaps we might let them go. But I would know their business and who they answer to."

"Then let me take four and ride after them," said Aegius. "We will kill if we must, but we may be able to scout out their position and purpose quietly."

Fen agreed, and in a moment Aegius and his scouting party—Wylla, Khaz, Sabian, and Eslow—were gone. This left the other five to the final stage of the cave work. They divided into groups: Fen and Liam in one, Xophnius, Tullian, and Thasperus in the other. They rode out bearing torches, for not only was dusk settling in but there was still the business of "Clearing the Caves." They doubled back across all the ground they had covered earlier in the day, revisiting every wall of freshly piled stone. At each, one man would dismount, light a bit of kindling from his torch, and pass it through a gap in the rock blockade, setting off a charge as he made quickly back to his mount.

They continued until they had revisited all twenty or so tunnels that had been discovered, explosive rumblings resounding at various intervals across the now dim landscape. This is, in fact, where the expression to "clear the caves" first originated—referring to one facing the worst with decisive and resolute action. (e.g., *He could no longer afford to take things casually but knew the time had come to 'clear the caves'.*)

It had been decided they would bivouac at a spot a few miles north of the caves where a small stream ran, and the scouts were to join them no later than the evening of the following day. So when the five had regrouped that night, leaving the eerie darkness of the caves and the threat of the mastids behind them, and returning to grounds more hospitable and alive, their hearts were light and spirits were high.

"I believe I will be telling the story of this day many a time," Tullian said as he slid off his horse and led her to the stream. "*Many* a time." He plunged his own head deep into the smooth surface of the water and scrubbed the filth off. He came up shaking his head with a spray in every direction.

Xophnius laughed a free-spirited laugh. "It is one worth telling, friend. Though words will undoubtedly fail to do the odor justice."

Thasperus looked over his befouled body then slapped his thighs with a hearty laugh that rumbled from deep in his belly. Then with one surprising plunge, he hurled himself into the gentle stream. The others burst into laughter and quickly followed suit as well. Shortly there were five men dunking themselves and each other in the cool dark waters and finding it refreshed them all body, heart, and soul.

When they had cleansed in the river and taken food for the first time since before leaving Ainsworth early that morning, the men took seats around the fire and settled down to a pleasant and thoughtful mood. Tullian, man of southern Winderlawk looked across at Thasperus, man of the north.

"It was a great thing you did... to come for this," he said humbly. "No one expected a northerner to care. Certainly not to come at their own risk."

They all pondered Tullian's words and the gratitude that so filled them.

Xophnius's voice lifted softly over the quiet group, "Brotherhood that is born by birth runs deep, but deeper the brotherhood that is bought with blood."

Like the aroma of just-baked bread hangs thickly in the air, his words hung just so over the men.

"I would stand with you," spoke Tullian to Thasperus. He then turned to Fen, who was reclining against the trunk of a willow tree to his right. "And I will stand with you. At any hour."

Fen gave a nod of grave appreciation, and Xophnius seemed pleased.

"You did well, Fen," said Xophnius, "very well."

And how things changed so suddenly from there it is hard to say. For at once, there was a dash from behind the tree at which Fen sat, and before anyone could do anything the figure of a man in a brown hooded mask had Fen around the neck and a black dagger point pinned against his flesh.

"Hold!" Xophnius commanded the intruder, and Liam was on his feet in a second but to do what he did not know.

"He has done well, you say," came the man's grimy and threatening voice. "You have no idea what you've done."

Fen tried to push against the man's arms, but his grip was solid and the dagger perniciously snug.

"What do you want," demanded Xophnius, considering every angle of the situation and secretly at a loss for the moment.

Liam scanned the area around Fen and his captor; there was nothing he could use against the man in one crazed rush at him. Tullian and Thasperus had no idea what to do but were desperate to do something. They looked to Liam for some kind of guidance and found a very unsatisfying blank expression in his eyes.

"I want nothing from you, old man," the stranger barked. "The life of this one will be enough when I have to give my reckoning." He jerked at Fen to drag him off into the dark, but the hostage kicked and pulled fiercely. Thinking it might be the only chance he had, Liam lunged for his sword that was on the ground an inconvenient distance behind him. But the man in the brown hood was not about to lose his prey. He drew his arm quickly to bring the dagger down as Fen struggled with every fiber in him; and before anyone knew what had happened, the body fell forward.

It was both bodies that fell forward, to be precise. It was Fen who crumpled on the grass as the body of his captor fell on him from behind, heavy and lifeless. A black dagger like his own was lodged in his back, and another hooded figure came out of the dark shaking, with raised hands, into the circle of breathless men.

He fell to his knees before them and lay his face on the ground, hands outstretched, palms to the sky. Liam was at Fen's side the next moment, pulling him up to his feet, and they all looked in bewilderment at the trembling man in prostration before them.

"What is this!?" snarled Liam at the quivering stranger. "Who are you!"

The man's body shook violently, but he tried his best to speak, "N-n-n-o one, sir." He sobbed, "I am no one. Only-ly-ly let me be taken from th-th-th-this place."

Fen took a step towards the man. Liam grabbed his arm to stop him, but Fen would not be restrained again. "Liam, shall we treat the man who saved my life as if he were the one who tried to take it?"

Liam's tone was angry, harsh. "He is one of them. Do not trust him."

Fen looked to Xophnius who wore the soberest of expressions but said nothing. Then looking on the mysterious and pitiful man weeping on the ground, Fen said kindly, "Rise, sir. Tell us your business."

Ever so slowly, the man pulled himself up so that at least he was on his knees. And there he sat, silently, face covered under the brown leather hood, head slumped miserably forward. But he did not speak.

In one hostile move, Liam reached for the man's hood and jerked it off saying, "Tell us who you are!"

And now it grew deathly quiet, for the men saw the face unmasked, and it was a sight for which no one was prepared. Tears streamed down the man's face—a face scarred too many times to be numbered.

"Fire and thunder," Fen gasped under his breath.

The stranger looked no one in the eye but simply hung his head again and tried once more to speak. "I-I-I-I want n-n-nothing. Only to be f-f-f-free of that p-p-place."

"You shall have it, friend," Fen promised.

"Commander!" Liam interrupted.

Fen looked at Liam sternly, "You do not know his story, and so you do not trust him. Perhaps that is right.

107

But if his story does not yet call for trust, it certainly calls for mercy. And he will have it here."

When there was order in the camp again, having carried away the one who had been slain and having cared for the new stranger with food and drink (which calmed and quieted the man considerably), they gathered once more around the fire and listened to his story.

"I am Oktahn," he began, so settled that his voice went as soft and smooth like the stream. "I was born in the Eastern Realms, the son of slaves who worked in the mines. There were thousands of us, sold and bought on the first day of every new moon... all mostly the business of mine owners and traders from the East. But on the day my time came—when I had turned twelve—it was not the usual buyers who came to the market that day. There was one man, and he bought us all. I had never seen the looks of one like him, skin dark and smooth, much taller even than the Barbarians of the East. Some of us he sent with his men to the North. The rest of us he took to the South. We were divided among many different stations. I do not know them all; I have done terms at many of them. We are moved every two years. In this way, we are unlikely to form connections with other slaves that might lead to a revolt. Some say there was an uprising in the Eastern mines once... a long time ago." A far-off look gathered like thunderclouds in Oktahn's pale blue eyes. He grew distant as if buried under a lifetime of painful memories.

"There was," said Xophnius quietly. His voice broke the spell over Oktahn. "A great uprising indeed, at the end of the Brumian Century." (You may not know that traditionally in the Four Corners, each century is marked by a name of historical significance to that period.) Xophnius looked pitiably at the tortured soul before them, and Oktahn smiled the faintest smile to hear that the legend was true.

"I was moved to the caves nigh two years ago," he continued his sad tale. "I was human before then. Or looked like one at least."

"Those are the marks of mastids that you bear?" asked Fen.

"Yes."

"What do you do at the caves?" Fen questioned further.

"We feed them," Oktahn answered. "Every third day the Murai brings a tonic that we must take down to the cave lakes deep inside."

"What is a Murai?" asked Fen.

It was Xophnius who answered. "Something of a chemist, something of a wizard... you will only find them in the Outer Regions. It is turning them poisonous, is it not," he said to Oktahn, more as a statement than as a question.

Oktahn grew visibly distressed but managed to say, "I do n-not know."

"You do know," said Liam. "Who sends you to the caves?"

"The overseers," Oktahn mumbled.

"And who do they work for?" Liam pushed.

"I d-d-do not know."

"What was the name of the man who bought you?" asked Fen.

"How c-c-could I know?" Oktahn stammered. "I see him maybe once in a year. He is called by the slaves Blade but only because he is dark like the weapons they give us to fight with. Who knows his name?"

"It is surely Kaineaux," replied Xophnius to the surprise of all, "one of Ahmahnric's warriors. He comes from a land far in the Western Wastes and is highly trusted by the traitor... and feared by all else. It has been many generations since Ahmahnric has given so much power to one of his own."

"You know him then?" said Fen.

Xophnius nodded, but Oktahn broke in nervously, "P-p-please. I want no trouble. We saw you. We s-s-saw you setting those fires in the caves. Junis said if we t-t-took you back to show them then m-m-maybe they wouldn't kill us." The fear in Oktahn's eyes began now to give way to a spark of something almost hopeful. "But when I was watching you I said to myself that I didn't know there was men that did great things anymore. And how could I let him kill you? I want no trouble and mean no trouble."

"Rest easy tonight, brother" said Fen. "You have many griefs to lay down."

Clouds had gradually rolled in across the sky, obscuring the sea of stars and moonlight that had lit the night. The fire was allowed to dwindle low as the men laid their weary frames out on the soft grass. Liam took a look-out position on the southern edge of the circle, next to the newcomer (as you might have supposed). But he needn't have worried about that man on that night; Oktahn slept the first real and proper sleep of his life.

It was difficult to say what time it was when Aegius and the scouting party returned the next day. A thick cloud cover persisted throughout the morning with not so much as a glimpse of sun, but perhaps it was somewhere near the noon hour when the party arrived. Aegius met directly with Fen and Xophnius to discuss their findings.

The three men walked a short distance northward along the river and took seats on the ground among a grove of willow trees that swayed rhythmically under a soft westerly breeze that blew.

110

"We tracked the raiders to lands twenty miles southeast of the Caves," began Aegius. "There is a fortress of sorts built into the rock there, much like a cave itself, surrounded by a compound of stables and structures where perhaps a few hundred men labor. It is several miles from the nearest outpost and seems to be something of a military base, though it is not guarded—or does not appear to be at least."

"Who is it to be guarded against?" replied Xophnius. "No one from the southern tribes has any business here, and a pocketful of individual rogues dwelling in the outposts pose no threat to a collective force at such a place."

"So if it is an army, an army to fight whom?" asked Fen.

"That would seem to be the troublesome point," answered Xophnius.

At this moment, they were interrupted. For Sabian, having washed and changed and seen to his horse, had then noticed the private gathering that was taking place; and he rather fumed at the idea of being left on the outside of it. Thus had he marched to the meeting of men among the swaying willows and waited until they had each turned to acknowledge him.

"Well," said he, "I understand *Commander*, that not all in our company are needed for such meetings of evaluation and planning, but let me say that *I* do not expect to be excluded from such senior advisory matters." His blond curls were wet still, giving somewhat the impression of a puppy that has just had its bath. Even so he held his head high and looked down on the men rather disdainfully.

"Fair enough, Sabian," said Fen. "What opinion do you bring in regards to the situation before us?"

The response caught Sabian off guard completely, as

111

he did not actually possess a well-formed opinion of their present situation. Being unprepared to answer the question intelligently, he simply sat down right where he stood and said, "Well, yes, let us discuss that. Please continue."

The men met for quite some time longer, though they arrived at only a few conclusions, which were as follows: firstly, Oktahn would likely be the most helpful source of information if it was determined that he could indeed be trusted; secondly, there was nothing really meaningful they could do at the moment being as few in number as they presently were. This lead them to the third conclusion, which was the decision to ride for Ainsworth first thing in the morning (since the hour was growing late) and once there consider how best to stir the men of Winderlawk to action.

Though a slow and light drizzle fell for most of the night, which made sleeping uncomfortable at best and nearly impossible for some, the sun rose bright the next morning. This alone cheered everyone, but also there was the joyful feeling of going home (excepting Sabian and Oktahn) after having accomplished a great feat. And the prospect of sharing the news that the mastid habitat and population had been veritably destroyed... well, one couldn't help but feel marvelously good about that.

They carried on light-heartedly as they followed the road north. Even Oktahn found himself with a bit of a smile every now and then as he listened to friends and brothers teasing one another or Xophnius telling humorous tales of various quests of misfortune.

Wylla had given her horse for Oktahn, offering to ride behind Khaz on the way back. Fen observed Oktahn in particular quite a bit on that trip, wondering to himself if their business at the Southern Caves would prove more meaningful to the entire Winderlawk tribe or to this single man with the marred face and wounded spirit riding beside him. The former slave said nothing as he traveled over the wide green hills of Winderlawk for the first time. Perhaps he hadn't realized yet or remembered that he was free to speak. Or perhaps he was too mesmerized by the way breaths of wind and morning sunlight work an enchantment over the soft grasses of the hills, sending a hushed whisper rippling through the shimmering blades- a sea of green alive in response to the air and light around it and over it and in it.

Whatever the case, he rode in peaceful silence, and the others rode in carefree exuberance, and it seemed possible to them that perhaps all wrongs in the Four Corners of the Earth might indeed be righted in time. Such was the hopeful spirit of those who rode into Ainsworth later that morning, but it would not remain so. And for some, it would be a long time before such hope was felt again. For the party reached the Lawk farm to find an enormous crowd gathered about, with long faces and grave eyes. There were northern Winn and southern Winn alike, and strangely a large mix of people who could not be recognized as Winderlawk folk at all.

"What has happened?" Fen mumbled to Xophnius, alarmed by what he saw. And then he had his answer. He saw Nora and her mother in the doorway, eyes red and faces streaked as it is for those who have cried all their tears only to find a fresh well of them again. And he knew.

12

A WORLD COMES TOGETHER; A WORLD FALLS APART

Everything was a blur—a chaotic, dark, senseless blur. There was the crowd gathered in front of the house, whispering to one another as they watched Fen stumble his way past them to the house. There was the pain on Nora's face as she tried to bring herself to look him in the eyes but couldn't. There was the helpless weariness that her mother Emaliys wore like a ragged, threadbare coat. There was Xophnius, making straightaway for the room where he had left Grable a few days earlier. And there was the sickening feeling as cannot be described by words.

"It was last night, Fen," Nora managed to choke out.

He stood there in front of her, nodding at her words and thinking vaguely of saying something like "thank you" for having been with him at the end; but his mouth was dry and his tongue was thick and "thank you" seemed like a strange thing to say. Anything seemed like a strange thing to say. Somehow his feet felt rooted to the floor, as if they were unwilling for him to see what must be seen. But he languidly forced one lead foot after the other past her towards the room. There was a burning in his throat, a sting in his eyes. He found himself blinking, blinking and shaking his head as if perhaps he could rouse himself out of this terrible dream. But no, there he was at the room, and there was the body laid out on the bed and covered with a pale sheet. And there was

Xophnius standing over him, arms raised, eyes closed, pronouncing a blessing of the ancients over the dead.

And what had he been thinking? That he would ride off to save the world and let the kindest of men who had been like a father to him die at home? Why had he let himself get carried away with this whole Resistance idea? A "commander." *Really?* The ridiculousness of it—the tragic, awful ridiculousness of it washed over him with its toxic waves of guilt, and he felt he might collapse there on the floor.

He staggered through the house, out the back and lifted his eyes to the small wooden bench that sat overlooking the eastern horizon… and to the tree that rose by its side, arms of bark branching out and leaves bright green from the abundant spring rains. It was beautiful and sad and lonely, and *what had he been thinking?*

He sat for a long time on that bench, apologizing to Grable in his mind a thousand times and swearing to himself that he would not be so foolish again. Nora watched him from the house, Xophnius beside her.

"He has no one," she said in a hollow voice.

Xophnius murmured the lines of some long-remembered Ahlrik sonnet:

"The one who dies
leaves behind
a loss that is not solved in time
for time
may only find
we loved them more than ever we knew."

"What do you think we should do?" Nora asked.

"Gracious, daughter, I should live ages longer and not know the answer to that impossible question. For what you ask most deeply is to take away his pain, and that is not the right of men."

Now, as Fen lingered on the old wooden bench—

feeling very lost and withered—and as his friends watched over him and took care of preparations for the burial, the masses remained assembled across the sprawling lawn and beyond. From the front steps of the house to the road, from northern fence-line to quite south of the house, men and women were grouped in various numbers, speaking in low tones or just waiting silently. Their presence, their identity, and their purpose will require some explanation.

Many of these were Winn. Some had heard astonishing reports about Fen; men who had been part of the mob at the Lawksbur had been wildly claiming that he was planning to ride off to the Southern Caves. And so, many had come to wait for the news of the returning party, finding sadly the bitter tragedy unfolded at the Lawk farm.

Others had heard first of Grable's passing, and in keeping with Winn custom, they had come to begin the three-day wake outside the house. Grable had been regarded as a kind, honest man, and many came to mourn him. It must also be said that the appalling news that mastids were now killing men had captured the attention and concern of Winn folk on both sides of the swamp.

To account for those among the throng who were not of Winderlawk, we must go back to the council at Ildiys. For the other Elders had been at work since then, to no small effect.

Kholrihk and Bryn had wasted no time but had hosted a banquet on the second day following the conclusion of the council. Among the scores invited were Kysmen noblemen (that being the twelve chiefs of the twelve wards of Kysmarc and a great number of the lords who owned and governed land within those wards), other prominent members of society, and a large number of carefully chosen younger tribesmen. These younger Kysmen called themselves "the Prophymas," an archaic Kysmen word meaning loosely, "those who declare change." (The Prophymas, at the time of our story, had been launching an outcry over allegations that certain nobles within Kysmarc had been negotiating trade alliances with the slave-trading Barbarians of the Eastern Realms. And in this suspicion they were not mistaken.)

And so those who belonged to the establishment of Kysmarc, so to speak, and those who were rising up from the next generation all came together in Ildiys, about a hundred and twenty of them. And they feasted in proper Kysmen fashion and then listened exceedingly long into the night as Kholrihk and Bryn bore witness to the rumors of Ahmahnric's rise and to the council's work in establishing a Resistance.

Now, it should be said that in Kysmarc, things like the true history of the tribes and of the Elders and such was still believed in some circles, most commonly in the kinds of circles as were present on this particular night. There were certainly some there who doubted very deeply that Kholrihk and Bryn were *literally* Elders from an ancient age or that there was *literally* an equally ancient enemy who had been conspiring against the Four Corners of the Earth throughout the centuries. Even these skeptics, however, esteemed Kholrihk and Bryn to be, at the least, sage and discerning Kysmen. And no one doubted that trouble—whatever the source—was brewing and should be handled appropriately.

As to the more controversial issue of *how* these rumors and threats to the peace of Kysmarc should be addressed, there were several opinions represented and discussed. A modest number were disinclined to do anything but would rather wait and see how things progressed over time, noting that sometimes these kinds of rumblings had a way of working themselves out, not unlike the unpleasantries of indigestion after a bit of overly mature goat cheese. "Things pass," as they say.

A much larger portion of the audience felt the idea of a formal Resistance movement was very much in order, particularly given the news that Dresdor was thought once again to be plotting some sort of quest for control over the other tribes. The idea, however, that it should be Winderlawk at the lead of this Resistance was almost as disagreeable to many of the Kysmen as it had been to Sabian Dresbane. The exception to this was the membership of the Prophymas, who tended to be more skeptical of their own kin—and consequently more open to intertribal collaboration—than the older generation.

In the end, all forty of the young Prophymas members unanimously committed themselves to the cause. Nine of the twelve chiefs and at least thirty-two of the lords agreed to it as well, pledging to rally as many as were willing in their domains. Another dozen or so pillars of Kysmarc society agreed to the same.

Some began the journey to Ainsworth the very next day. Others were longer in setting the affairs of their homes and businesses and families in order. Thus it was a stream of Kysmarc men that flowed over the next week towards the rolling farmscape of Winderlawk, amassing outside the Lawk farmhouse and growing in number by morning and by night. By the hour of Fen's arrival, it was a solid number of one hundred sixty-five, and it continued to swell in the days that followed.

There were very few Ahlrik at the Lawk farm when the company returned from the Southern Caves, but that was only a matter of timing and not of interest or willingness. The Ahlrik, on the whole, have never lived a minute in a hurry and can be counted on for their speed in much the same way the days can be counted on to pass quickly when it is the end of one's school term or one's birthday is looming ahead on the calendar.

When Phlycia had returned to Ahlred from the talks in Kysmarc, like Kholrihk and Bryn she also went to work spreading the news from the council among her tribe. But of all the tribes, things in Ahlred happen, perhaps, most uniquely.

First, you must understand that the land of Ahlred is densely wooded almost in its entirety, and this landscape is as much a part of the people as anything is or could be. Towering conifers, massive hemlocks, and enormous maples whose foliage turns the autumns into a botanical ocean of crimson... the forests of Ahlred are a magical, mythical wonderland.

And living amongst the wonder of it all, from the forest floors to the canopy tops, are the Ahlrik. The idea that a tree would be cut down to make space for a house is, to an Ahlrik, as preposterous and disdainful a thing as one could imagine. Instead, their dwellings make use of the trees themselves, typically (but not always) having their foundations on the ground and stretching up skyward around and among the leafy world. They are not "treehouses," mind you, in the common sense of the word, for they have proper walls and roofs.

There might be anywhere from two to eight trees growing within an Ahlrik dwelling, trunks supporting the structure of the house, branches serving all sorts of wonderful purposes. Thin ones might be rafters in the "ceiling" of the house, with lanterns or light globes hanging down from them. Thick ones might have smoothed tops and serve as reading benches or even tables.

Most often Ahlrik dwellings are built in communal clusters known as Boreal Fraternities, each one

119

encompassing, on average, perhaps twelve to fifteen homes. And in these fraternities it is as common to see the upper levels of homes connected by a network of bridges as it would be to see ground level homes connected by sidewalks or streets. For each Boreal Fraternity, an individual man or woman serves as the leader and spokesperson for that group. This person is known as the Torchbearer and is selected by each fraternity every seven years.

Phlycia's own dwelling, Cloudhaven, was nestled in the very heart of Ahlred. Here, because of the elevation and rise in the earth and the breathtaking height of the trees, Phlycia's uppermost rooms were actually nestled among the clouds themselves. The size of the dwelling was in its height not its width or breadth, each level being a very modest size. And a pulley-lift of sorts ran from the ground to the celestial, tree-top observatory.

The system of summons and news among the Ahlred is very ordered and well thought out. Each Torchbearer is responsible for signaling a certain number of other Torchbearers, who in turn, inform the Torchbearers designated for their respective fraternities, who in turn do the same, and so forth. In this way, news may spread throughout the whole of the Ahlred tribe in five or six days for matters of little urgency or in as few days as two when it is of a serious nature.

All of this is to help you understand that when Phlycia returned to Ahlred, her first task was to summon the Torchbearers to the Northern Round at Cloudhaven. Just a very short walk from Phlycia's home, an amphitheater had been created in the northern slope of the rise. And on the second night following the summons, the torchlight could be seen winding through the dark forest, rivers of fire as the Torchbearers came making their way to the Northern Round (as the outdoor theater was called).

Watching the men and women streaming in, Phlycia stood before the rounded slope of seats on a wooden stage that was built out among some of the lower-lying branches of a large elm tree. By 10 p.m., virtually every Torchbearer in Ahlred had arrived, hundreds of them lighting up the night with torch fire as had been done so many times at assemblies throughout the ages.

As has already been stated earlier in this story, in all the Four Corners of the Earth it was the Ahlrik who held most loyally and completely to the history of the tribes, to the sacred Writings of the Elders, and to the restoration of Kembarius's heir to the throne. So when Phlycia spoke of the threat of Ahmahnric and of the Elders' call for a Resistance, unanimous agreement went up easily among the Torchbearers. And then she shared that a young Winn from southern Winderlawk was charged as Commander, and the mood changed.

"One of the *unbelievers?*" asked Plymean, quite senior among the Torchbearers, and a murmur of assenting voices echoed quietly around the theater.

"He is the man for the hour, friends," Phlycia replied graciously. "You have the discernment of the Elders to vouch for him."

"But how can a Winn be trusted to uphold the ancient truths?" Plymean persisted. "Are we to believe he has completely rejected the age-old skepticism of his tribe? Is he truly a man the faithful of Ahlred can follow?"

The calm and orderly crowd sat very still waiting for Phlycia to respond, and she did not find the words immediately. When she finally did, her voice was warm and motherly yet undeniably strong.

"Friends, I cannot promise he is everything you

121

would like him to be nor what you might expect him to be, but do not despise him for his unlikely beginnings. He is not yet all he will be, and I say again: he is the one for the hour at hand. Of that we are confident."

It is not common for the Ahlrik to believe the best about the unbelievers (as they are prone to calling the other tribes— especially the Winn), but equally if not more so, it is against the Ahlrik to *disbelieve* one of their own, particularly Phlycia, the highly trusted and deeply beloved Elderess of the tribe. So there was not much more to be debated, for she had announced Fen's command with unequivocal certainty, and those gathered were left with the decision to honor her judgment or not.

When the vote was cast and the decision to join the Resistance was found to be unanimous, the Torchbearers dispersed immediately to share the news with their fraternities. Only a handful of the southern-most dwelling Ahlrik had arrived at the Lawk farm by the mournful day of Fen's return from the Caves. But like the men of Kysmarc, their numbers grew steadily.

This accounts for all but the Dresden, and you will surely guess that they were by far the most hostile and opposed when they received the news that Huros had for them. Sabian's band of loyal men dwindled from thirty to sixteen or so almost immediately, and it is unclear whether those sixteen who reluctantly agreed to journey to Winderlawk did so out of a commitment to the Resistance or out of concern that their Dresden brother had been brainwashed and was in need of deliverance.

Sabian had wished to travel straight from the council at Ildiys to the Principal City, Valdestria, before joining the others in Winderlawk so that he might speak with his men face to face. But the Elders had proposed that if he journeyed at once with Fen and the company, it might communicate more effectively to those back in Dresdor his commitment to the Resistance and the urgency of the situation. In the end Huros was pleasantly surprised that as many as sixteen were willing to travel to the backwards farmlands of Winderlawk to join Sabian.

Sabian himself was shocked to find them waiting at the house when he returned from clearing the caves. He had nearly convinced himself that no one would come, and the sight of sixteen Dresden brothers huddled together on the outskirts of the crowd nearly brought tears to his eyes.

Obviously the outsiders who had come to the Lawk farm were completely surprised by the sobering circumstances they found upon arrival. They had been expecting a muster of sorts and instead discovered they were part of a mourning ritual. Word spread quietly among them all on appropriate behavior and expectations concerning the Winn tradition for laying to rest those who have passed on. And as newcomers arrived throughout the days, their tribesmen respectfully passed along news of the situation.

For three days there was largely silence in and around the farm, as is the Winn custom for a wake. This three-day period is concluded with the burial of the dead and speeches by the family. By the morning of burial there were nearly seven hundred people gathered outside, though Fen was completely unaware of this fact. When he had risen from the wooden bench late that first night, he had gone directly to Grable's room where he had remained for the entirety of the second day of the wake. Nora had asked if she might bring him something to eat (though fasting is commonly the practice during the mourning rites). He had declined.

When he came out of the room on the morning of

the third day he found the house, as he thought to be, empty. He was bleary-eyed and fog-headed. Not having slept the previous two nights nor having eaten those days, combined with his wrenching grief, he felt hollow and weak. He tottered out of the room looking for he did not know what, but he stopped upon hearing voices coming from a small sitting room just down the hall to the left.

"He deserves to know," came a familiar voice—it was Aegius.

"He is in no state of mind to bear that news," replied another. Fen vaguely recognized the rich voice of Xophnius.

The voices were a bit jumbled though in his weary mind. He steadied himself against the wall, tilting his head towards the direction of the voices without a thought as to whether or not he was eavesdropping.

"If you do not tell him," Aegius was saying in a low and serious tone, "then I must."

"It would seem you are a man full of all kinds of revelations, are you not?" Xophnius retorted scornfully.

"That is not fair," Aegius replied. "He does not bury a kind man only; he buries a father. And he ought to know it." There was a long pause, and then Aegius spoke again, "You know I am in the right."

Fen's brain was reeling. What was going on? What were they saying? Certainly they were talking about burying Grable, but… Fen could not force order to his chaotic thoughts. Xophnius was saying something now.

"Curses," he said wearily, "I know it. This will bring everything to the light whether he is ready for it or not."

"Whether who is ready or not?" It was Fen who appeared in the doorway and whose voice was quite unexpected by the two men who had been having what they thought to be a private conversation. "Are you talking about me?" he asked with a suspicious look in his dark eyes.

Aegius and Xophnius exchanged a brief look of understanding with one another, and Aegius stepped forward gently. Reaching for Fen's arm he said, "Why don't you sit, brother…"

But Fen shook off the man's hand and took a defiant stance. "No, why don't you tell me what you two were talking about?"

"We will tell you everything," said Xophnius, "but let us bring you something to eat first—"

"Xophnius!" Fen's voice was shaking in anger.

"Why make this harder than it must be, friend!" Xophnius urged. "You are weak and tired, and there are impossible things that must be borne. At least put some bread in your stomach before—"

"Was Grable my father?" Fen demanded. Tears were brimming like pools, and his voice was hoarse even as he tried to will it to be firm.

Without hesitation Aegius answered. "Yes."

13

WAR RESOLUTION

While the world seemed to be unraveling for one young man in Ainsworth, something quite significant was also taking place at the same time in Dresdor. In Valdestria, Parliament was in session, which meant that fifty seats ought to have been filled with fifty men who were to be discussing various issues related to Dresden law and order.

Fifty men were not present however. One of those seats belonged to Sabian Dresbane, who had been mysteriously absent more than a week. In addition, for three days now, nine more seats had been vacant. These, as you may have supposed, belonged to men who had listened to Huros and followed after Sabian to Winderlawk.

Pertius Mindóhr sat down in his well-cushioned chair and looked miserably at the vacant place next to him, where his closest friend should have been sitting. Sabian's things were all neatly arranged on the desk: his writing kit with a leather bound journal of parchment, a scrolled atlas of the Four Corners, and a desk lamp. Its shiny copper base was fitted to a beautifully crafted crystal globe inside of which was one smooth ivory candle with trimmed wick.

Where was he? Pertius wondered. Winderlawk, Huros had said, but where exactly? And for how long? And doing... what? Had the others reached him? Pertius should have gone himself. He had argued for it, but

Huros had all but forbid it, saying that someone had to stay who would keep the Norians from completely running over Parliament. But he felt it deep inside—he should have gone.

While he was lost in thought the morning period had started with the Parliament Speaker's opening remarks; and when his name was called in the long succession of names he answered as he always did: "Pertius Mindóhr, here for the representation of Saldawn Region and for the good of Dresdor."

Dozens of other finely dressed men seated at small writing desks in straight rows across the room answered similarly, "Harton Rhoove, here for the representation of Liymna Region and for the good of Dresdor"; "Exilion Dreslowe, here for the representation of Khorly Region and for the good of Dresdor." And so forth.

When roll had been called the Parliament Speaker invited the Chancellor to address the Representatives. Chancellor Aymes, a short and stocky fellow with a gravellish voice ascended to the podium which stood at the head of the room.

"My colleagues," he began, and Pertius found himself rolling his eyes without thinking. Of all the men in Dresdor for whom he had lost all respect, Chancellor Brohmar Aymes was at the top of the list. He did not come from an especially wealthy family, but Pertius had noticed several curious improvements in the man's financial affairs over the last few years. Foremost of these was the Villa at Gars Landing where he now resided. How Aymes had come to afford one of the most sought after properties in the Principal City itself was unexplained. Pertius suspected it was somehow related to the tight bonds he had formed with several of the prominent Norians in the city. Aymes conveniently agreed with virtually everything that these foreigners proposed. That such a snake happened to be the sitting Chancellor of the Parliament was rotten luck.

Chancellor Aymes retrieved a paper from his coat pocket and unfolded it carefully. Addressing the room he said, "I bring a sealed proposition from the office of the Regent."

Yes, yes, very well, thought Pertius. Dresdor was the only one of the four tribes who had anything like one central leader who presided over the whole tribe. This was the Regent, and when Parliament received a sealed proposition from his office, nine times of ten he was asking Parliament to approve a new tax of some sort.

It had been quite a while since the last proposition, so it was indeed probably about time to be asking people for money again. The most recent tax had been instituted a year ago to finance the construction of a dam in one of the eastern regions where flooding had been troublesome. Pertius wondered what this proposition would call for; he could not remember any issues having been discussed as of late that might call for such a thing. And then his mouth fell open; the Chancellor's words rung in his ears like sirens.

"And so it is with the soberest of mind," Chancellor Aymes was reading the Regent's letter, "that I call upon this venerable and auspicious Parliament to consider the greatness of this tribe, the nobility of her past, and the promise of her future. I call upon you to take up the cause of the tribe's rightful rule, forgetting not that troubles abound within the Four Corners of the Earth that would be lessened if not resolved were the other tribes to find refuge under the protective wing of so great a mother as Dresdor. However, knowing what is best for oneself and having the courage to embrace it are not always the same. This have we seen in past years. To their shame, Ahlred and Kysmarc and Winderlawk would

128

sooner face certain ruin than submit to Dresden rule. But let us not allow their naive and prideful thinking to run our course. Were the tribes more reasonable in their nature, perhaps an agreement for governance over them could be reached peacefully. But history has shown the futility of this. If the tribes are to be united under Dresdor, they shall have to be brought under rule forcibly. Thus do I present to the Parliament this War Resolution, calling for your full support and approval. For the good of Dresdor, for the good of the kingdom. Wilmore Dressihks, Two hundred and thirty-ninth Regent of Dresdor."

"Outrage!" cried Pertius. "This is an outrage!" He had flown to his feet and was met with many commands that he control himself and that order be maintained. Pertius ignored them. "War Resolution!?" he exclaimed, "We are a full ten less in this room and you would have us vote on war with that number?!"

"Sit down, sir!" the Parliament Speaker commanded. "If you have a motion—"

"If I have a motion?!" replied Pertius. "Yes, I have a motion! Let us not send the troops of Dresdor on the abominable mission of attacking our neighbors unsuspectingly and unprovoked! That is my motion!"

The room was fairly lit on fire with energy, most of which was working against Pertius. The majority were calling for the vote, eager to approve the Regent's proposal of war. But there were certainly a handful of men who either were not sure about the matter or were set against it as Pertius was.

"The Regent has called for a vote, and vote we shall," Chancellor Aymes said firmly.

One of the few other dissenters spoke up now, "Pertius is right. We are too few to consider such a weighty resolution. We must wait for a full house before we may consider this."

"Nay!" shouted several of the men. Over half the room were on their feet now, shouting at one another and arguing passionately one way or the other. The rest were respectfully demanding that order be restored and that men sit down and proceed in a manner befitting their station.

Pertius would not yield. He stood at his desk with fire in his eyes, scanning the room. He took note of the six Norians who held Parliament seats; it was not surprising that they all looked quite pleased. No doubt they had urged the Regent to make the most of it while so many dissenters were absent.

Presently one of them by the name of Benriys stood, fingered a curious ivory whistle hanging on a chain about his neck, and raised it to his lips. Blowing its shrill tone over the shouts and cries in the room, he effectively silenced all of them by the sheer surprise of it.

"Fine sirs," he began. "It has been an honor of the highest order for me to serve among so excellent a company for the common good of so extraordinary a people."

Applause broke out in the room. Pertius could feel his blood boiling inside. How could so many here have fallen under this pathetic sort of spell?

The foreigner continued. "When I first came to Dresdor, I was overwhelmed by the enlightened nature and surpassing industry of this place. And I asked myself, 'What might the Four Corners of the Earth be like if only this kind of progress and prosperity might be spread throughout?'"

Cheers and applause erupted more passionately, with more than a few rising to their feet in hearty agreement and appreciation of his words. Benriys motioned for calm though and finished his remarks. "Yes, it strikes me unfortunate that so many of our colleagues are not here for this momentous occasion. But this I find even more unfortunate: that their love for Dresdor is so diluted that even though they have been endowed with the privilege of membership in this house yet they fail to uphold their duty." His eyes singled out Pertius with an unmistakable look of satisfaction.

"That's right!" shouted one man in the front row. "It is their choice to be gone when there is business to be done! Vote!"

"Let's have the vote!" echoed voice after voice.

From here things ran away like a train. The Speaker was calling for the vote and men were writing their positions and casting their ballots. The room seemed hot and still, and it was hard for Pertius to breathe for a moment. Before he could make sense of things, the Speaker was reading the verdict, "Those who approve the Regent's proposition are thirty-six. Those who oppose are four. The War Resolution passes..."

His voice trailed off as Pertius rose weakly from his chair and stumbled his way out of the room. Huros. He must find Huros. What Pertius did not notice was Benriys slipping out quietly after him.

The sun was high in the sky by the time Pertius and Huros had come together at one of the frequently used secret meeting points. By making use of the catacombs under the city streets, one was able to reach the wide River Gars well outside the city limits, where a stone bridge crossed the quiet waters. The bridge was substantial and also hollow in its construction, so that several men, approaching it from beneath along the river's edge, could tuck themselves away behind the stone edifice of the bridge wall.

Pertius was a sore mess—out of breath, his hair disheveled from his hands that had run through it a hundred times in gestures of dismay. The collar of his shirt was askew, and he paced wildly between the stone walls of the bridge. Huros tried to calm him.

"It is done, Huros!" Pertius said in an alarmed whisper. "The Resolution is passed. They will go to war and who knows what will follow." His hushed voice echoed off the rock.

"They say they will go to war, but that is still to be seen," Huros said calmly. "There may yet be something to stay their hand."

"Wishful thinking," Pertius said miserably, running his hands through his blond, unruly hair again.

"It is a concerning step for certain," said Huros, "but all is not said and done yet. Let us think and act quickly."

"I will get word to Sabian," Pertius said decidedly. "They must know what is coming."

"And I will see what I can do here," said Huros. "The High General of the Dresden Forces is a fair man and a friend. I will speak with him this night; I think it quite possible that he will not rush the troops to battle under the circumstances. And I will see what others may be won over for the Resistance; it may be that this War Resolution may push some to our side."

Pertius stopped his pacing and looked at Huros gravely. "I will join them in Winderlawk?"

Huros thought for a moment. "I believe you should. You will likely not be safe in the city any longer. I myself will join you in Ainsworth when I see that I have gathered whatever last bit of support I may here."

The men arranged a few other details and parted ways. Huros followed the river away from the city towards the residence of High General Lyhnge. Pertius, on the other hand, made his way cautiously back to the catacomb entrance just down from the bridge, where a tunnel opened into the rock face of a low series of cliffs that banked the river there.

Stepping into the stone passage, a clipping sound from his boots echoed unfortunately in the chamber. Pertius winced and paused, feeling very unsure of himself for a moment. He told himself to keep going, refusing to let his nerves run away with his courage. The clipping echo resumed as he quickened to as brisk a pace as he could manage without breaking into an all-out run.

Suddenly, there was something else in the echoes. Footsteps? He stopped abruptly. Maybe his ears had tricked him. He heard nothing at the moment and told himself once again to move on, but before he took another step there it was again. Yes, footsteps. They were coming from the direction before him; he would turn around.

No, there were more—these were from behind. How could someone be coming from behind him? Unless they had been hiding—waiting for him—when he entered the tunnel. He urged himself to *think, think*! Perhaps it was a coincidence, random travelers crossing paths in the catacombs. But he knew it was not. And his heart sank as the sound of footsteps drew closer.

"Who is there?" he called out boldly, willing himself to at least appear fearless.

"Pertius," came a familiar voice from the dark ahead. Benriys, he knew it instantly. A moment later the Norian had rounded the last bend in the passage separating the two and was standing before Pertius. Footsteps continued slowly from behind.

"What are you doing here, you odious crook?" Pertius questioned defiantly. "Are you not busy, what with all of your work to send my kinsmen off to war?"

Benriys scoffed. "Yes, I am busy. And my work is all the more because of you and the Dresbane and all of your lot who feel you must stir up the people against what is bound to come."

But for the lanterns that were hung sparingly at long intervals, the catacombs were dark. Deathly dark. And it was only a very dimly lit shadow of the Norian that could be made out by Pertius. He squinted to sharpen his focus on the foreigner's long face. The footsteps behind drew nearer still.

"'What is bound to come?'" Pertius echoed. "You and I have different ideas about that. I believe you Norians must be exposed and outed from Dresdor. That is what I believe is bound to come. You are trouble for the tribe."

"Well, I am trouble for you today, sir, that is for certain."

The footsteps stopped behind Pertius, and he forced himself to look slowly over his shoulder, his feet frozen where he stood. Looking this direction he easily saw the dark, massive shadow of a man against the dim glow of a lantern behind him. Turning back quickly to Benriys, he made up his mind then and there. He stood up a bit straighter and drew his shoulders back, lifting his head high.

"You claim to be for Dresdor, but I know better. The truth will come out in the end, and it will prevail against your corruption." Pertius spoke with passion and found that somehow in that moment he actually felt as fearless as he wished he were.

Benriys shook his head solemnly. "I will leave you to work that out with Kaineaux. He seems to think otherwise."

With that, he turned and disappeared into the dark passageway from which he had come, leaving Pertius to face the shadowed figure behind him.

Kaineaux's voice was angry and foul. Even so Pertius found some inner strength coursing through his body, pumping through his veins.

"I have come to deal with you directly, worm" the huge man spewed.

"You say it as if perhaps I should be honored. Forgive me if I am not," the young Dresden replied brusquely.

Kaineaux unsheathed his blade and stepped towards Pertius who was unarmed but not unclear concerning what was about to take place.

"Your 'Resistance' is a child's game against a force you cannot begin to match. Ahmahnric will crush it, and all will be his."

Kaineaux was right before him now, and Pertius looked him dead in the eyes. "We will see," was all he said.

Kaineaux did his unholy business and turned to leave, speaking to the body that now lie crumpled on the stone floor, "But you will not."

14

THE RISE OF A KING

Beneath the stables at the Lawk farmhouse was a musty cellar, not used for much the last few years. On the last day of Grable Lawk's wake, just a few hours before burial, seven persons were gathered there; these were Xophnius, Aegius, Liam, and Sabian, as well as Nora, her mother Emaliys, and of course, Fen.

Having had some porridge and coffee that Emaliys had prepared and persuaded him to take, Fen was feeling a bit more solid but his mind was still spinning. To have not known one's father and then discover you had lived all the time with him, and—what is more—now it is too late to know him as you might have… it was a stone hard lot. But Fen was doing his best to suppress the anger that surged and begged to be released in wild torrents. He kept quiet when he felt he could not trust himself to speak well, and he looked to Nora more often than not. There was a peacefulness about her that somehow whispered true things and soothed him.

The hatch door was closed for privacy, but the room was lit abundantly with lamp light. There were a few wooden stools, some old farm tools that were in need of repair, and several empty barrels scattered around the otherwise bare and stuffy room. The women were given the stools and the men stood or perched themselves on barrels, and as soon as they were settled, Xophnius looked to Aegius with a nod of encouragement.

"We grieve with you, brother," Aegius started

sympathetically. "The loss of Grable is the bitterest of news. That he was your father is, no doubt, the strangest of news. And the more that must be said now will be no less astonishing."

The room was so quiet that one could have heard the beating of a fly's wings. Nothing stirred. Liam sat in a corner staring vaguely at a crack in the earthen wall as if looking long past it into time and space beyond. Emaliys and Xophnius both watched Fen keenly, the first with a motherly tenderness and the latter with discerning focus. Sabian, Nora, and Fen were fixed on Aegius, who stood before them looking thin and worn.

"I was ten years of age the year you were born, Fen," said Aegius. "Always will I remember it. It was my first year to manage the planting and harvesting myself. And the last year with my father."

Fen hung on his words, sensing a tangled story knotted up in them. Liam remained lost in some other world, and Aegius carried on.

"When Grable and Westerlyn learned that they were expecting a child, Grable insisted that your mother go into hiding until you were born."

"Hiding?" Fen asked.

"For her safety, yes," replied Aegius. "With her went my father and brother as well as Madam Wrenvale." He nodded to Emaliys.

Fen looked questioningly at Nora's mother whose eyes were glassy with tears. "I don't understand..." Fen began.

"Your mother was the heir, Fen," Aegius said. "She was of Kembarius's royal line. My father had been guardian over her for years, and his father and uncles before him, just as they had watched over her father... we have always watched over the heir."

"The *heir*? Did you know?" Fen asked Emaliys.

"Your mother and I were the best of friends since we were babes. Yes, I knew."

"Did you?" Fen turned to Nora, but he knew the answer before she could even shake her head. The wonder and confusion in her eyes said it all.

Aegius continued. "Ahmahnric has come very nearly to the brink of destroying the royal line at numerous points over the ages, but the Order of the Watch has preserved it to this day... where you now sit."

'*Where you now sit*'... those words sunk deep into Fen's heart, in some way the long lost answer to a thousand questions. *The heir?* To a throne—to a kingdom? *Him?!?* Fen Lawk, who had known of no parents, no family line, no history... how was this possible? And yet didn't he find himself sensing it to be true somewhere deep inside?

Emaliys now spoke gently, "Your parents wanted to keep you a secret. They knew the danger you would face if Ahmahnric were to learn of you, as has happened in the past. It was a cold, end of winter day when we started out for Ahlred where my kin lived. There were four of us making the journey: your mother and me, with Aegius's father Broughston and his eldest son Rehdmohr. We were to stay there until your mother gave birth, and then she and I were to return to Winderlawk with Rehdmohr to look out for her. Broughston was to stay with you at the house of my sister. It had been arranged that she would care for you 'til your second year and then bring you to Winderlawk. Grable and Westerlyn had planned to share with their friends the sad story that they were unable to have children of their own and then happily receive you as an orphan who needed a home."

Aegius broke in at this point, "Thus there would be no public records of Westerlyn Lawk's child and no one who knew she'd had one."

The wooden door to the hatch creaked and rattled as a wind blew over it up above, but no one took the slightest notice. There was something almost sacred being unveiled, they felt; and it was utterly captivating… in different ways for each of them.

"But she did not come back from Ahlred," Fen prompted, "nor your father and brother." He looked at Aegius with a heavy gaze.

Aegius wore the pain of that memory on his face as if it were a wound raw and piercing. "No, they did not come back."

"You were but nine days old," said Emaliys, "and Westerlyn was still very weak from birth. I feared for her, so I had gone for the Healer who lived an hour to the east on the banks of the Mullen. I had been there only moments when I saw the smoke. Everyone on the river saw it."

Emaliys took a slow breath and wiped the tears that had escaped. Aegius stood with eyes closed, unknowingly shaking his head back and forth ever so slightly, as if perhaps he might will it to be untrue.

"Men and women from all over rushed to help," she continued. "The whole fraternity was ablaze before we had got there. And crawling out of it with you in his arms was Broughston. It was confusing, people were shouting and crying and running in every direction. The smoke and the heat were unbearable. Broughston was covered in black, as were you, but he put you in my arms and swore me to shield you with my life. Then he went back into the blaze to look for your mother and Rehdmohr." Emaliys looked at Aegius with sparks in her teary eyes. "A *great* man, your father."

Aegius lifted his head and stood up a little taller, and something beautiful in her words swallowed up a bit of his sadness that had been born on that day in his tenth year.

She looked next to Liam who remained transfixed in his own thoughts and a thousand miles away from anyone else in that cellar.

And now Sabian spoke for the first time, his eyes wide, "Do you mean to say you think he is King?"

"That is precisely who he is," answered Xophnius. And then he added, "Or at least will be, when he is crowned."

Questions poured from Fen about all of this new revelation; among them was the need to know what—or who—was to blame for the fire that stole so much that day.

"No one knows how it started," Emaliys replied. "By the time you were born it was the end of summer, hot and dry. It is the season when such tragic accidents may be seen in the wood."

Xophnius seemed to think otherwise, "But also is it true that Ahmahnric's raiders have used such methods against the Ahlrik for generations."

Emaliys nodded, acknowledging that possibility as well, "Who can say for sure? Grable was beside himself and feared that it was as Xophnius has said… that perhaps Ahmahnric had heard rumors of Westerlyn, rumors of you. He traveled up to Ahlred to take you back home in his own arms and never told a soul who you were. He was going to tell you though." She sighed deeply. "And even though he may not have told you in life, he has at least told you in his death."

Outside the cellar in the world above, the throng of people was beginning to stir with the restlessness of the last few days. If you ever have taken part in the Winderlawk mourning rites, then you know how the days of fasting and somber quiet begin to wear on a person, giving way to a roused, almost energetic atmosphere towards the end of the third day. There was more chattering and reflections or questions murmured than there had previously been, and though no one spoke in a particularly loud voice, the collective sound of it all was quite a buzz.

Khaz and Tullian led a group of six men in preparing Grable's body for the burial. And perhaps you are wondering about Oktahn in all this. Consider that it would not necessarily be overreaching to say that the man who was to be laid in the ground had died from the work of Oktahn's own hands. One might be willing to weaken such a statement by noting that he had not chosen the work for himself, as it had been forced upon him; Oktahn himself was not inclined to make such allowances.

He felt keenly the brutal point that a good man had liberated him from bondage only to meet with this kind of pain and loss *because of him*. It *was* his fault. Who could say otherwise? If he closed his eyes but for a breath, he could feel himself in the dark deeps of those caves. The dank stench of the place was somehow in his nostrils even now without warning, and he spit instinctively as he had done a thousand times in those caverns.

Perhaps freedom, for him, was a mirage. Perhaps he would never truly escape the darkness of his chains. Perhaps, in fact, he belonged back in those caves, with the other foul creatures of this world. These were the kinds of thoughts that had occupied Oktahn for the last few days as he sat alone in a field some distance from the house itself.

He could go back South, but just the thought of it made Oktahn cringe, almost cower. There was too much horror in going back and too much shame in staying here. Where did that leave a person?

141

It is indisputable that guilt and shame are slave masters of the most heinous class, and how one will respond under their yoke cannot be predicted.

The hour of dusk was approaching, which is traditionally the hour of burial. Back in the cellar, Fen's thoughts were beginning to stray from this whole shocking narrative back to the reality that he was to lay his father to rest shortly.

"I thank you," Fen said, walking to Emaliys and taking her hand, "for your friendship to my mother which has carried on all these years in your care for Grable and myself." He turned to Aegius and to Liam who was behind him, "And I thank you, though such words are miserably small weighed on the scales against what you have given. Madam Wrenvale tells the tale of your father and brother—men who gave themselves up for another—and I learn from them what it means to face the darkest hour as a true man."

At his words Aegius bowed his head and replied, "A man does not hold his own life above the life of his king. It was only right," and looking up with something like joy in his blue eyes he added, "Your Majesty."

Those two words lit the room with a moment of wonder. Nora found that she was crying quite without knowing when she had started or exactly why she was for that matter. Xophnius looked more at ease than she had seen before, and her mother too seemed to have discovered a peace in speaking the secrets she had so long borne.

"Will you…" Sabian started meekly, "that is, all these people here… should we…" He was unsure why he could not bring himself to ask outright if the people gathered there were to be told of Fen's rightful kingship. If he had possessed the courage to be painfully honest

142

with himself, he would have admitted that coming from nearly the highest ranking family in Dresdor, he had dreamed as a little boy (and even entertained the notion once and again in his adult years) that perhaps he might find himself in the position of uniting the four tribes and being asked to rule a kingdom—in the absence of a true king at any rate. It had not been unthinkable. But *now*— now, as things turned out, it actually was unthinkable. And the reason he was stammering was that he was trying his level best to slay his most daring boyhood fancies while, at the same time, carrying on with business; and that is almost always impossible.

"Do you mean are we to tell everyone that Fen is the heir of Kembarius?" Nora finished Sabian's question for him.

"It does not fit," Fen said, "that people should come to bury a man in one breath and be told they have a king in the next."

"However," replied Aegius, "Hundreds here did not come for a burial. They came to join the Resistance under your command, and your throne strengthens the cause."

"Xophnius, what do you think?" Fen looked to the man who had begun slowly pacing the room.

"I think," he answered, "that ages ago in the twilight years of the Dogstar Century we faced much the same dilemma. Having found the heir, the Elders moved swiftly to install him as king. But the people were a long way from wanting to fall under the rule of a king in those days. If you have read Kholrihk's writings on the matter, you will know the situation did not go well. There was a violent uprising, and the heir disappeared."

"Though not to us," Aegius noted quietly, to which Xophnius gave a slightly belligerent huff.

"Was that the Revolt of Valdestria?" Nora asked, so pleased to have before her a living version of the histories she had read so voraciously all her life.

"Indeed," said Xophnius. "Indeed."

"Liam, you have not shared your mind here," said Fen.

Caught off guard by the attention, Liam gave a weak smile. "I am not the one in this room to make such decisions."

"Well then," said Fen, "I agree with Xophnius. If I can lead well in these days, it may be that the people will see a king they want to follow when they are told the news that there *is* a king they *must* follow. Let us wait patiently for that time."

When they rejoined the world above, they found the wind blowing in a soft rush against their faces. It was the kind of wind that smells of things wild and fresh, that rustles in the leaves and stirs your blood and makes things come alive… that sort of wind.

And that evening when they buried Grable Lawk, Fen buried alongside him a lifetime of questions and wonderings and unknowns. And from the ashes of it all, began the long-awaited rise of a King.

15

BATTLE PLANS

The whole place was alive with activity and surging with anticipation the next morning. Many of the Winn folk had left the previous night following the burial, but some others had stayed on, out of curiosity if nothing else. In addition, others had continued to arrive, and all of this left the crowd somewhere around a thousand men strong on the lawn of the Lawk farmhouse and eager for what this new day might bring.

While everyone was anxious to hear what the unlikely young Commander might have to say, Fen had insisted that the first order of business when it came to the troops was to feed them. Tullian's wife, Melindrah, along with their elder daughters and the boy who was hired to work in the fields—they had all been working feverishly over the last few days in preparation for this. There were monstrous pots of porridge that had been brewing since well before sunrise, trays upon trays of biscuits, and bucketfuls of boiled eggs. The younger children had spent the last few days gathering berries from the plentiful thickets around the edges of the Lawksbur, and they watched rather proudly as the bushels of their labor were grabbed up eagerly.

Granted it was not the most impressive of offerings, but there's nothing like days of fasting to make simple porridge and boiled eggs taste fairly wondrous. Meanwhile, Fen and those chosen as his senior counselors had taken the house as a command post, and at present were meeting with Huros who had just arrived.

"I suppose you have heard the news from Pertius," he began.

"From who?" asked Fen.

Worry gathered in Sabian's face. "We have heard nothing from Pertius. Is he not coming himself?"

Huros sighed a mournful sigh. "If he is not here by now..."

Huros related to the group all the news regarding the vote in Parliament on passing the War Resolution. It was alarming to say the least- for Sabian doubly so. That his friend was missing under the circumstances left a sinking feeling inside him, and he did not jump into the talks as the others did. There were several questions and concerns put forth at once, but Fen silenced them, looking at Huros.

"Do we know where they will attack first?" Fen asked.

"I spoke with the High General just before I came," answered Huros. "They seemed to know that you are gathered here in Ainsworth and are making their plans to come."

"And how do you suppose they came to know that?" asked Xophnius.

"I truly cannot say," Huros replied. "Yes, I spoke to several men following the council in Ildiys—men who refused to join your company in Winderlawk. But I cannot see that a single one of them would have had any part in revealing your location. Having spoken with High General Lyhnge, I find it puzzling how much they seem to know."

Aegius walked briskly to the windows that were open to fields north of the house, pulling and latching the shutters.

"Should we believe someone is telling them?" he

146

asked in a low voice. They looked around the circle at each other— Xophnius, Sabian, Aegius, Liam, Huros, and Fen.

"You have not said much, Dresden," said Liam.

Sabian looked confused and then angry as he realized what was being implied. "If you think I have in any way compromised or betrayed information—"

But Liam interrupted him, speaking matter-of-factly. "Is it not worth noting that you are the only one of us with ties to Dresdor, and that this Resistance fell sorely short of meeting your own expectations?"

Sabian's face flushed with fury, and he rose proudly to his feet. "I have never been so insulted in all my years. I am of the House of Dresbane. We do not lie." Passion was escalating in Sabian's voice. "We do not sneak secrets like gypsy rogues. That my honor should be questioned by the likes of *you...*"

Now Liam stood as well to meet Sabian's defiance, but Fen spoke firmly to both, "Pax, brothers." Liam and Sabian each stared cold at the other as Fen continued, "Sabian has given no reason that we should think him disloyal. I do not think the situation calls as urgently for suspicion as it does for focus and resolve, for which I depend upon both of you."

Tempers simmered downwards, and the two men resumed their seats at the round wooden table.

"What else did you learn from the general," Fen asked Huros.

"I think you will see them in less than a week. And they will certainly outnumber you greatly if your numbers do not sharply increase," said Huros. "Lyhnge is a man of reason and restraint, and I do not think him exceedingly supportive of the Resolution. But he is also a soldier and a commander of soldiers who will certainly discharge the duties given him by the governing authorities of Dresdor.

If he is given the mission of conquering you, you may expect him to fulfill it to his last breath."

"And this is what the people of Dresdor want?" asked Aegius indignantly, "Conquest over all?"

"Not entirely," answered Sabian. "We are not quite so barbaric as that. You will find that most common people have no interest in going to war for such a thing. Though many of them do believe Dresdor will rule again one day, they know that battle has proven a failure over the ages; and they are not eager to send their sons and husbands to die for a cause that has been so long futile."

"It is those in power whom the Norians have enchanted," added Huros, "It is the Regent's ear they whisper in; it is the governors and Parliament members whom the Norians buy with extravagant gifts and promises of greater power."

There was a knock at the door, and Aegius slowly opened it. Wylla and Khaz entered with Oktahn between them. His head sagged apologetically on his shoulders, and his eyes locked onto a wooden peg in the floor near the corner, eager to avoid seeing anything of the men there. What he wished even more was that he might avoid being seen by them.

Certainly they had brought him in here to mete out his punishment. Fortunately, in no way did they seem to be like the overseers of his past. Instead of brutality, they held a dignity about them; possibly there would not even be a flogging. Perhaps they would simply put him in prison. He deserved at least that. However, it was also not impossible that his sentence might be death. He studied the planks in the floor, considering that possibility and feeling the fairness of it weigh down on his very bones.

"What gave you two the idea of bringing the likes of him in here?" asked Liam, obviously displeased.

"I did," replied Fen.

Liam gave a stiff nod that was somewhat apologetic. "Forgive me." His voice was dry, and he eyed Oktahn with unmistakable disdain.

"I want to know about the slaves in the Southern Deserts of the Outer Regions," Fen began, looking at Oktahn, "the locations where they are based, how great is their number... you could help us with some of those questions could you not?"

Oktahn could not help but lift his eyes from the ground to the man who had just spoken such unexpected words.

"S-Sorry?" was all he could manage.

"The slave bases in the South," Fen replied. "If not all, you know about many of them, yes?"

Aegius leaned in close to Fen, "But we must focus on the threat from Dresdor this moment. There is no time to spare crusading in the south."

"On the contrary," Fen answered him, "the problem of Dresdor may very well be helped by what we learn of the South."

All attention was turned on Oktahn, and the poor creature with the mangled face and blistered spirit just stood there bewildered.

"Oktahn, can you help us?" Fen asked with an increased gentility, sensing some great disturbance within him.

"You w-want me to help you?" Oktahn asked in a pitiful sort of way.

Liam mumbled something indiscernible in Aegius's ear. Xophnius and Huros exchanged doubtful looks, and Sabian's gaze drifted off as inwardly he returned to the worrisome disappearance of Pertius.

Oktahn surprised them all when, looking solidly at Fen, he spoke in a strong steady voice, "I will tell you everything I know."

For a full hour Oktahn, indeed, poured out everything he knew about the Southern Deserts and the slave stations hidden away in them. He told the men about the fortress Aegius had scouted with the others. Crowbane it was called, and it was one of the largest stations. Several hundred slaves were kept there at any given time, where they were drilled in combat training as well as put to work building weapons with nyloth ore that they received in shipments sent from the North.

While most of what Oktahn said seemed consistent with what Aegius had seen himself, he was surprised to hear that as many slaves as that were kept there. But Oktahn explained that the fortress inside the rock was far larger than he had assumed, with hundreds working in the dungeon-like chambers.

He told them of the smaller, more eastern-lying stations that sent out raiding parties, primarily for gathering whatever supplies or horses could be gained through stealing. These bases housed slaves who had earned a higher ranking than others by proving to the overseers a certain level of both cruelty as well as allegiance.

Then of course, there was the station near the Caves from whence Oktahn had fled. They were around a hundred in number there and were made to work the fields (if they could be called that) and, in turn, take their shifts in the Caves. There was little to be farmed in such a dry, infertile region, but at this station there were black potatoes and crescent beans grown to supply a number of the bases. Even with the task of hauling water from miles away and the grueling heat of the sun, field work was always preferable to shifts in the Caves. Twelve slaves had died in the last year from the mastids, Oktahn said.

He avoided looking at anyone directly at this point.

How stupid of him to mention that, as if there was any need to remind them how deadly the mastids had become. He changed the subject quickly, speaking about the overseers—how there were many of them but relatively few armed guards at any of the stations.

"Fen, what is your purpose in all this?" asked Xophnius.

"I am wondering if we could not negotiate a sort of... revolt. If we sent Oktahn with a number of our men to Crowbane, perhaps he could spread word among the slaves. With so few armed guards, it would seem we could overthrow the fortress with not a great effort. Those who wish to run for their freedom would be allowed to do so. But those who wished to fight back against Ahmahnric could join us."

"Do you think it wise," asked Sabian, "to build an army out of slaves? Can we expect any kind of integrity? I fear they will look out for themselves and leave us when it proves convenient."

Xophnius studied Oktahn curiously. "I wonder what you have to say about that. Can the slaves be trusted?"

"Some yes, some no," Oktahn replied quietly. "Same as all men I would think."

"Indeed," smiled Xophnius.

"Then will you go?" asked Fen.

"I will do anything you ask, sir."

It was decided that Oktahn and a party of thirty men would leave for Crowbane that very afternoon, purposing to reach the fortress in the dark of night. Liam volunteered to lead the mission, clearly anxious to keep an eye on Oktahn.

If things went as well as could be hoped, Oktahn would be able to slip in inconspicuously that night, targeting those slaves whom he might know or gauge to be most helpful to the cause. They were to have the next day to spread the word amongst themselves, with the riot planned for that night.

Additionally, the council of leaders all felt it plain enough that riders would have to be sent to the far northeast where the Norians lived, to see whatever might be learned firsthand of their true purpose.

"If we spend the horses," said Sabian, "we can make Valdestria in two days. With fresh mounts I believe another two days could have us in Nor Que Pneuris."

"Even so," replied Aegius. "Four days going, four days coming, not to mention time that is taken there… we do not have it before Dresdor is on our doorstep."

They all fell quiet, considering the situation. And finally Fen decided.

"We have no choice. We must know more about who the Norians are and if they are, in fact, working Ahmahnric's schemes against the tribes. Sabian should go, of course; but, Huros, you have only just come—I feel I cannot ask that you should turn and leave at once."

The large man stood slowly and grinned, deep lines curving and creasing at the corners of his smile. "You needn't ask when threat demands. Besides, at this point in my life, a few days' ride does not seem so long."

Xophnius could not help letting out a chuckle, and then a voice surprised all the group.

"I will go too."

It was Wylla. There was some initial mumbling by the men that did not seem to make any distinguishable statement, and Aegius looked keenly at her with something less than fear but more than concern.

"I can ride faster than all of you—excepting perhaps the ancients," she nodded at Xophnius and Huros. "And should there be trouble on the way two is a dangerously small number. There is more strength in three, yet the number may still move quietly without attracting attention." She paused, observing the uncertainty in their faces. "My horse is ready. When shall we leave?"

Huros seemed quite satisfied, but Sabian looked to Fen with anything but confidence in his eyes.

"All right," Fen finally said. "Huros will go with Sabian and Wylla. And we will pray the wind of Elethas carries you all the way and back."

So the three riders to the North left, unaware how providential it was that their number had increased and how disastrous it would have been had it not.

And the riders to the South gathered their company and prepared to leave as well, hoping to liberate and add to their number, completely unaware of what was to unfold there.

16

TRAITORS OLD AND NEW

"The tribes appear to be banding together against Dresdor... they're calling it a Resistance."

A fire crackled in a circle of stone inside what appeared to be a cavernous chamber. Torches lined the stone walls, casting a golden orange aura across everything. Though the setting might seem unrefined, the furnishings inside were surprisingly well appointed. Several chairs of dark leather were gathered round a table of gleaming black metal, nyloth in fact. And shined as it was, it sparkled in the firelight and was smooth as glass.

Fine dishes and platters were pushed aside, suggesting a meal had just been finished. But it was not many who had gathered and feasted. Rather, only two had come to this solitary chamber, as they often did, to discuss matters of the kingdom.

One was Kaineaux, who had spoken moments earlier. He sat in the chair just right of the table head. And the man who sat in *that* chair was none other than Ahmahnric himself.

He sat as an emperor might on a throne, the flickering light nervously illuminating his smoothly shaved head and the sharp lines of his nose and chin and jaw. Unmoved he was, by the news Kaineaux brought. Instead, Ahmahnric raised his goblet and swirled the dark red liquid inside, watching it catch glimmers of torch light. He savored its smoothness for a moment before responding to Kaineaux.

"A Resistance?"

Kaineaux gave a subtle nod but said nothing.

"Seems amusing. Rather surprising honestly—that they would come together— and yet pathetic all the same. What else have you learned?"

"I will know more in the coming days. I have a man inside now."

Ahmahnric seemed quite pleased with that statement and shook his head piteously, "It does not bode well for them if they already have men willing to give their own up, does it?"

"A worthless lot," Kaineaux answered with disgust.

Through one of the heavy, hinged metal doors a man began to enter, thinking he would discharge his duties of clearing the table.

"Leave!" Ahmahnric commanded without so much as a look to the man. And he scampered away as a dog might with its tail tucked between its legs.

"There is only one possible concern," Kaineaux stated hesitantly.

Ahmahnric sat back in his chair, not in a relaxed sort of way but rather in a resolved, calculating sort of confidence.

"There are a few in Dresdor who are siding with the Resistance. It is *possible*—though not likely—that the War Resolution might be upturned in the end. In truth, the tribes are not standing against Dresdor as much as they imagine they are standing against you. There is the smallest of chances that Dresdor will be won over by the rogues and stand with the other tribes."

Ahmahnric laughed a genuinely honest laugh.

"Oh, poor Xophnius and Huros must have been busy telling all the evil stories of 'Ahmahnric the traitor.' I am surprised they found any audience at all for those ancient fairytales. For men who have been given limitless futures, they are so idiotically fixated on the past."

He laughed again, condescending and arrogant.

"Yes, lord," said Kaineaux, "but it does remain that if all four tribes do fight together, it is uncertain if we have the force to defeat them. I think we may, but I cannot say with certainty. I will know more when I hear from the rat."

Ahmahnric's demeanor shifted back to his vile and dour air. "Are our troops ready for battle?"

"The Barbarians and the Slaves, almost," Kaineaux answered. "The Norians have been delayed with issues in Dresdor, but it is days only before they can march."

"Well," Ahmahnric replied disdainfully, "if the poor creatures decide to band together, we will simply divide them again, will we not?"

******

Far south, beyond the border of Winderlawk and well into the Outer Regions, Liam, Oktahn, and their company of men were approaching Crowbane. It was a clear, crisp night, though no moon to light their way. This was preferable, as they were grateful for the concealment of darkness. Liam and Oktahn rode at the head of the group, Oktahn looking the slave no different than all his years before, though he waited to put on the leather hood until he must. Eslow rode also beside them. Aegius had been keen that someone who had already scouted the fortress with him should go along. With Wylla having headed north with Sabian and Huros, this had left Eslow and Khaz only, and Eslow was eager to rise to the call.

They rode three abreast, making as little sound as possible, until they came within sight—or what would have been sight had they more than starlight by which to see. Crowbane was now a vague mishmash of distant shadows and forms in the direction straight ahead of them. The company halted.

"All right, you," said Liam to Oktahn. "I give you no more than two hours."

Oktahn looked at Liam in a panic. "B-but I was to have the entire night to find men. What can I d-d-do in two hours?"

"We will wait here, and you will return within two hours. You will tell us everything you have done and everything you have said. And if your story seems believable we will give you the rest of the night to finish your work, and we will move into our positions."

"But that m-m-means I have to make it in and out twice. My chances of being d-d-discovered—"

"You were able to sneak up behind the neck of the Commander without being noticed. I'll wager you'll be fine."

Liam's words stung, taking Oktahn back to that night at their camp by the stream. He wanted very much to point out that he had not been the one to do any violence to the Commander. But what was that worth? Truthfully, had he not followed Junis there to do exactly as Junis had, in fact, tried to do? And had it not been only at the last moment that he found some strange strength within him to act so differently than they had planned? He realized at that moment that he would always be distrusted and despised by free men.

He looked at Liam and said nothing. Then he dismounted, pulled on his hood, and began creeping steadily westward, that he might approach the fortress from the point he had chosen around its side.

"That seemed perhaps a bit harsh," Eslow said softly.

"Let him earn his place, I say." Liam's voice was cold.

The men waited in the darkness. There was neither

wind nor sound of creatures as one might find in that part of the South at night—rock badgers, hissing locusts, or the desert loons. It was utterly still.

The time was nearly up that had been given to Oktahn, and the men began to wonder if Liam truly would abandon the mission and march them all back to Ainsworth in the dead of night.

Liam turned to Eslow, "Tell the men to mount up. We are leaving."

"It cannot have been two hours full yet," pleaded Eslow. "And the Commander is counting on us returning in greater number. How will it be if we return with one less instead?"

"How will it be if we return not at all because he betrays the whole lot of us?" snapped Liam.

And then the two men were interrupted by the faintest sounds of someone approaching. Out of breath, he removed his hood, and there in the darkness appeared the shape of Oktahn.

"Well, then?" said Liam.

"I think favor is with us," Oktahn answered. "Almost at once I found six who I knew. When I told them our plan to overthrow this place, they all agreed. They are already spreading the word as we speak."

"That is good news," said Eslow, relieved.

"They say there has been talk of war coming which has many of the slaves anxious," Oktahn added. "They think that will lead more to revolt than might have otherwise."

"War?!" said Liam. "With who?"

Oktahn shrugged.

"A lot of men we can expect to add to our ranks from a bunch of slaves who are only joining us to *avoid* war," Liam said smugly.

"Maybe you are wrong," replied Oktahn, surprising

the men around him. "Maybe it makes a difference to a slave whether he is fighting for the men who keep him in chains or whether he is fighting against them. I mean, they are only slaves, but I think they know the difference."

There was a tense moment of silence before Liam finally responded, "Fine then." He addressed one of the Kysmen who was standing nearby, "Grimwell, you will take your men around the west side. Eslow, you and your men will remain in this position; I will take my number around to the east. Oktahn, get inside. We will watch for your sign nightfall tomorrow."

They all immediately dispersed, Oktahn back the way he had come and Grimwell and Liam's groups filing away in opposite directions. Eslow turned to the nine men in his keeping.

"Well, we have the rest of the night. We should at least sleep while we can. I'll take first watch, who will take second?"

The following day was a lesson in patience for the twenty-nine men who waited outside Crowbane. They tried to busy themselves with thinking through possible challenges that might arise that night and how they would deal with each one, but it did not seem to make the minutes pass with any greater speed.

Beyond the western perimeter, quiet conversation eventually sparked amongst the men posted there. Between the ten of them there were four Kysmen (Grimwell having already been named as one of them), five Ahlrik, and one Winn.

"If anyone had told me I'd be standing a post in the Southern Deserts of the Outer Regions one day with a bunch of Ahlrik and a soul from Winderlawk... I'd have told 'em to have their daft head checked," remarked one of the Kysmen with a bit of a chuckle.

"Aye," said a serious looking fellow from Ahlred. "That I should see the day I'd be riding side by side with a bunch of..." He stopped there.

"Bunch of what?" spoke up the lone Winn present. "With a bunch of unbelievers? Is that what you were going to say?"

"You've said it," the Ahlrik replied. "And if it's not true then how is it that so few of Winderlawk's great men are present when rumors fly that Ahmahnric is about to rise against the tribes? Where are all the men of Winderlawk, friend?" The edge of his tone and the bite of his words were obvious, and the Winn rose to a challenging stance without missing a beat.

"As best I remember, one of them is Commander of you and the rest of us and this whole blasted thing. So there's one of them."

Grimwell spoke in a placating manner, "That is enough. We are not enemies here. And we did not come to fight each other."

Round the eastern side, Liam's men entertained thoughts much along the same lines though none of them dared to speak them aloud, knowing full well Liam would tolerate none of it.

They all, save Liam, were lying about with whatever cloth they might have to shield their faces from the blazing sun. Around noon, Liam called one of the men to his side. Straining his eyes toward the distant fortress he asked, "Do you think those are guards walking about that exterior?"

"Oh I could not tell from such a distance, sir," answered the man. "Could be guards, could be slaves, could be overseers... could be anyone I suppose."

"Well, we need to know," Liam replied.

"I do not know how—," began the man, but Liam

interrupted him.

"I am moving in for a decent look. I do not trust that Oktahn is telling us everything."

Several of the men started up at hearing these words, and Liam instructed them, "It is hours till the signal. I have more than enough time to go and see more what their position really is. Go nowhere until I return."

"And if you do not return?" demanded one young man—one of the Prophymas from Kysmarc.

"Then do what you can to meet up with the others and make back for Ainsworth." With that Liam turned to go, but another of the group pressed the matter further.

"And how do you expect to go unnoticed moving in so close?"

Liam smiled. "My life has afforded me good practice in moving about unnoticed." And he was off.

You may imagine how uneasy and nervous the men had grown when sunset was approaching and Liam was not back. Because the riot was to begin by the slaves themselves inside the fortress rock—clearly not visible to the men of the Resistance, Oktahn was to signal that the riot had begun by hurling a blazing torch into the air. Upon this sign were all three bands of men to ride in swiftly.

Depending on how many slaves had agreed to revolt, the remaining work of capturing the overseers and guards would be potentially minimal. With slaves numbering in the hundreds and overseers in only the dozens, no one had expected much likelihood of any serious backfire with the plan.

The sun was sinking shyly in the west with every passing moment, and dusk was settling over everything like a gray film. All the men at the three posts were mounted by now, knowing it could be any moment. Eslow and Grimwell's men to the north and west all watched Crowbane for the torch to fly. In the east, Liam's men watched just as eagerly, but more than the torch they waited to see their leader on the horizon.

"Where is he?" one asked impatiently.

"And what if the torch goes up and him not back?" said another.

The horses sensed the nervousness of their riders and fidgeted as well.

Of course neither Grimwell nor Eslow had the slightest idea of Liam's absence, and so they did not worry about what they would do at the moment they should see the torch. They simply waited, some with swords already drawn, ready to ride in.

Sadly, they did not see a torch. And in the confusion that followed, decisions were made that proved poor, though the blame may hardly be laid upon them. For what happened was this.

Liam's men at last did see their leader, running as if the fire of Elethas was on his heels. As he drew near they could hear his shouts, "TRAP! We must ride! It is a trap!"

His men saw his meaning and sheathed their swords preparing to flee. The young Ahlrik who held the reins of Liam's horse rode forward to meet him, and Liam leaped up into the saddle the moment he was within reach. And they saw. They saw what looked perhaps a hundred men charging out of Crowbane on horseback, with weapons raised and voices shouting.

"You all go!" shouted Liam. "I will ride for the others. They have surely seen and are already in flight. But I must be sure."

The stampede of hoofs and shouts of voices was growing louder with each second.

"I will go with you!" insisted the one Dresden in the group.

"No!" Liam shook his head. "I'll not risk anyone

else's life because of that traitor. All the way back to Ainsworth. Now go!"

The eight men all spurred their horses into a northward gallop, while Liam headed west.

Liam was partly right, both Eslow and Grimwell had indeed seen the charge coming out of Crowbane, but he was also partly mistaken in that neither group had fled. Indeed, neither had known they ought to—that is, until it was too late.

Both groups were equally perplexed when first they saw the riders emerging. Were these slaves who had overthrown their captors and were riding wild for their freedom? But why had Oktahn not signaled? Perhaps he had been struck down before he had the chance. Or perhaps he had not been able to for any number of reasons. Was there still a struggle for control going on inside the fortress? Were Oktahn and the others waiting for the help that had been promised them?

By the time these questions had been considered and weighed, there was no more time. A decision had to be made. Eslow addressed his men quickly.

"They are likely escaped slaves who mean us no harm, but we must advance on the fortress as we promised. There may very well be men fighting for their freedom inside and waiting for us."

Grimwell had made similar remarks to his own group. And so it was that twenty men rode valiantly towards the treacherous slave base as they had promised. However, the force that was charging towards them was not as they had estimated.

When all was said and done, nine only returned to Ainsworth, where Liam informed his Commander that twenty lie fallen at the mouth of Crowbane... and that Oktahn was nowhere to be found.

17

THINGS UNEXPECTED

Two hours more till Valdestria. The horses galloped mile after mile. Every bone and muscle in Sabian's body screamed for relief. Wylla felt the same, though the sun would have grown cold and fish begun to fly before she admitted to it. And to think that Valdestria marked only half the way to Nor Que Pneuris. Sabian tried to fix his mind on something else. Anything else. Thus, presently, when Huros called for a halt, he was met with no objections from either of his companions.

They reigned in the horses and eased them slowly to a pond Huros had spotted. "Pond" might perhaps be an optimistic label, but nonetheless it was a pool of water for the steeds and a moment of rest, even if only a few minutes' worth, for the riders.

"They will be cared for well when we get there?" Wylla asked, patting her steed whose muscles twitched and jerked under her white coat. Wylla untied her leather flask, allowing herself just a bit of water. Huros had lain down on the grass almost immediately and closed his eyes.

"There is no one like my man, Rusa, when it comes to horses," Sabian answered. "She will be like a new beast, when next you see her." He smiled reassuringly at Wylla, and she was relieved at his words. "I must say," he added, "in no way did I expect a horse of her size to keep up at such a pace. She is remarkable."

His honest compliment took Wylla by surprise. "Yes, she is."

Sabian turned to Huros, flinging sweat from his blond curls as he did so. "I suppose you'll want to enter the city from the north, where we are less likely to be noticed... make our way back to my place?"

Huros neither moved nor opened his eyes but answered, "That was my thinking, yes."

"Surely, though, you do not intend to sleep the night there?" Sabian asked further.

"No, we dare not spend a moment more than we must in Valdestria. It is the horses, and then onto the next stretch."

"I believe Huros may indeed be sleeping his night as we speak," Wylla said with a smile.

"I'm doing nothing of the sort. I do not really believe in sleep anymore," Huros said good-naturedly, rising to his feet and gesturing that it was already time to move.

Minutes later they were pounding the road to Valdestria again, and a few hours later they were approaching the northern perimeter of the city while the sun was dropping quickly to the west.

The northern district of the city was always less crowded than other areas. It was almost exclusively residential, and even as far as that went, it was only for very affluent members of Dresden society. The three riders were very pleased to find the streets as quiet as they had hoped they would be.

When they reached the large gate with the shining Dresbane crest on it, they were let in immediately—that is, Sabian and Wylla were let in. Huros, contra his earlier remarks, had decided he *would* risk a few minutes extra that he might try to learn what had become of Pertius. He would meet them on the north side of the River Gars within the hour.

"Lord Dresbane," the gatekeeper bowed as he shut the gate behind them. "You have been gone some time, lord. We... were not expecting you."

"Thank you, Niyls," replied Sabian quickly as he and Wylla dismounted. "It's quite alright. I'll not be staying."

Sabian led Wylla around to the back of the house with their horses, with the gatekeeper Niyls following awkwardly behind them. Here a gravel walk led through sprawling gardens to a beautiful stone stable. Hearing steps behind him, Sabian turned back to his gatekeeper briefly.

"It's alright, Niyls. I have no need of you. I'll just have Rusa help with the horses."

Niyls halted nervously and appeared unsure of whether to leave or not, but this hesitation went unnoticed by Sabian and Wylla who pressed on toward the stable. Neither did they notice when Niyls did not, in fact, go back to his post at the gate, but rather hurried to the house itself and slipped inside.

When they reached the stable a minute later, Sabian was displeased that Rusa was nowhere to be seen.

"Honestly..." he muttered under his breath.

But Wylla responded, "As he said, you were not expected. Why don't you go look for him? I can take the horses inside and get started with them."

She led both horses through the wide-arched stable entrance. *Prince's ponies,* she thought, *this is the nicest place for a horse I've ever seen.* She had only just got inside and was letting Sabian's charger into an open stall, when she heard his voice outside:

"There you are," he was saying, to which she heard another man's voice reply greetings and apologies in very servile tones. She wondered if she should continue to undress the horses. *Of course he'll have his own way he likes things done here*, she thought to herself. And she turned to join Sabian and leave the horse work to his groom.

At first all she saw was Sabian and a man, whom she at once took to be Rusa, facing each other just a few steps beyond the stables. But it was only a moment more till she noticed the man who was not quite walking—more like creeping—towards Sabian from the direction of the house behind him. And then she saw the glint of the blade in his hand.

"Sabian!" she shouted fiercely.

He wheeled her direction, alarmed but unaware of what danger there was or where it lay. The man from behind made a wild attempt to close the gap, lunging at Sabian with his knife. The next moment, a cry was let out, but it was not Sabian. Better said, the *worst* of it was not from Sabian, who was indeed struck but fortunately only slightly in his right arm. His attacker had missed his mark due to the arrow that Wylla had released two seconds after she had shouted Sabian's name. It had lodged in the man's chest near his right shoulder and had taken him to the ground.

Clutching at the slash in his right arm, Sabian spun to see his assailant. Wylla had another arrow already nocked and kept a steady eye between Rusa and the house as she took a few cautious steps towards Sabian and the man on the ground. He was writhing in his pain and muttering furiously under his gasps of breath.

"Why, Benriys," said Sabian, as if the words gave a foul taste in his mouth. "I was not expecting to find you in my house."

Though he could not manage words at the moment, Benriys kicked a cloud of dust and gravel at Sabian and spit. He grabbed the arrow to break it and pull, but Sabian put a boot on his right shoulder. Benriys wailed for mercy.

"Who else is in my house," Sabian demanded, not yet relenting.

"No one, no one!" he swore then adjusted his reply, "Niyls! He warned me you were here. But there is no one else. Now help me! *Please.*"

Sabian turned to Rusa with a pained look, "I did not think your loyalty so cheap." Rusa started to shake his head as if to deny that he knew anything about it, but Sabian stopped him. "Sit! Right there. Am I to believe you did not know he was coming for me?"

Rusa, realizing his guilt was indisputable, sat on the ground miserably and began actually to weep. Wylla was now at Sabian's side, her weapon at ease.

"Time, Sabian," she whispered quietly.

"I know it," he agreed and looked angrily at Benriys. "I did not have time to deal with an ambush at my own home today. So here is my offer for you; consider speedily. I am leaving this place in seven minutes. If you answer my questions plainly, I shall extract that arrow honorably and send aid to your cowardly self here when I have gone. If you are not so inclined, I shall tie you up as you are in that stable like a beast. Now, I want to know who the Norians work for. What is your answer?"

Benriys was enraged but desperate, caught in a hard situation. The pain in his chest was crushing, and as much as he loathed Sabian, he sensed his life depended that moment upon his help.

"We answer to Kaineaux," he mumbled and then coughed gruesomely from his wound. "He is Ahmahnric's man. Now help me."

Sabian moved not the slightest. "Why the war? What does Ahmahnric gain if Dresdor rules the tribes?" Benriys groaned a laugh that sent him coughing again. Now he found that he did not mind answering the questions so much; informing the young Lord Dresbane of his coming demise felt rather satisfying actually.

"This war is only the beginning… the tribes will tear themselves to pieces while Ahmahnric has marshaled a force from all over the Outer Regions. Did you know that?" Benriys looked with great pleasure up into Sabian's serious face. "No, I think perhaps you did not. Well, you will know it when they come in and finish off what is left of the tribes. Ahmahnric will rule, you poor fool—not Dresdor. And the people of the Outer Regions will live like kings in the Four Corners."

Sabian responded with poise on the outside (though truthfully Benriys's words were unnerving to say the least), "Well then, that settles the matter of our bargain." He reached down and had the arrow extracted in moments, in a manner none too rough though Benriys cursed and sputtered as if the victim of the sorest brutality.

"Wylla, on the bright side, it seems we may have more time than we thought," said Sabian. Then he turned back to Benriys. "Now, as to the matter of you sneaking into my home and the violent attempt on my life (with my own blade no less), this will suffice." And with that he reached back down and plucked both the ivory whistle and chain that was always at Benriys's neck, along with the cream-colored linen cloth that was tucked in the pocket of his tunic.

It was fully night when Wylla and Sabian at last met up with Huros on the lapping banks of the Gars. Sabian felt that night that he had acted honorably in sparing Benriys's life, a choice he hoped would not prove foolish.

When the sun rose on the Resistance Camp in Ainsworth the next morning, quite a lot was already going on. Kholrihk and Bryn had arrived the middle of the night, bearing the unsettling news that Dresden troops had been sighted crossing the Medius and would likely reach the farm by nightfall tomorrow or perhaps the following day at the latest.

Huros had sent brief word to Xophnius that they would not be continuing on to Nor Que Pneuris but instead would be returning directly from Valdestria with grave news. Certainly it was futile to speculate about what they had learned, though inwardly everyone did.

There had been a very early morning meeting to discuss these items, after which Fen had dismissed himself and gone traipsing through the busy camp. Of course Aegius went with him as he always did now.

It was a very different scene from the peaceful Winderlawk farm it had always been. Between those who had come, all sorts of supplies and materials had been brought to Ainsworth, which were now unpacked and deployed. Tented pavilions had been erected and extra makeshift corrals built from timber that had been cut and hauled from the Lawksbur. Hundreds of horses now filled them.

Few of the men had ever seen battle. They were farmers and businessmen, gentlemen and woodsmen— not primarily soldiers. A portion of them, however, did have some training, and a few of the very oldest among them had actually taken part in the last conflict between the tribes. That had been nearly forty years ago now and, in the end, had accomplished little else besides nurturing the many hard feelings between the tribes.

All around, men looked up as Fen walked past, trying not to stare too conspicuously at their young Commander. He was the source of many questions murmured amongst the men. Even now two Ahlrik paused over the arrows they were fashioning, one whispering to the other, "What do you know about him?"

His companion shook his head and shrugged. "No

more than you. They say the Elderess believes in him highly. And I'd not take her opinion lightly."

Fen and Aegius had just passed by them when a young Dresden nearby ventured to join their conversation.

"Did you hear about what he did at the Southern Caves?"

They had not, in fact, heard any such news, being relative latecomers; and the account of the event seemed to make a positive impression on them.

"I heard about it from my own kinsman who was there with him. 'Pluck and wits he has'—those were his words."

"Let's hope so," the first Ahlrik answered back.

As Aegius and Fen reached the southern perimeter of the camp, Aegius read the disappointment in Fen's eyes.

"Did I not tell you, Commander? He is not here or we would know. I am to be informed the minute his face is seen."

Fen wore the discouragement and concern over Oktahn's absence plainly.

"Do you believe it, Aegius?"

Aegius sighed and shook his head wearily.

"No," pressed Fen, "I need to hear from you on this. Do you really believe Oktahn betrayed us at Crowbane?"

"I am not sure what else can be believed," Aegius replied. "Someone did, it would seem... and he is inconveniently the one who went in and who is now absent."

Fen nodded reluctantly. "I just... something in me cannot accept it."

"He has had the world against him all his life. It has made him... not right, perhaps. He can hardly be blamed for that." Aegius grew serious and deliberate, "And yet actions such as treason cannot be excused either, whatever personal tragedy may have unfolded in his life."

"I know it," Fen answered heavily. Then looking up at the sky, he noticed how late in the morning it was getting. "I am on my way to see Nora now. I assume you can give me a bit of privacy. For a personal conversation?"

Aegius smiled. "A *bit*."

Nora had gone to the school that morning and was still there looking through a book when Fen and Aegius arrived, though students had not been coming for some time with all the troublesome events and concerning rumors recently.

"I suppose we'll just have to consider school closed until things quiet down," she said with a sigh as Fen and Aegius entered. "Is there any indication when that might be?" But she shook her head as soon as she said the words. "An impossible question, I know. Ridiculous. Please forget I said it."

She closed the book she was holding and walked over to a shelf in the corner. It was made of wide wood planks, each one supported by an oddly shaped clay pot at either end, and stacked four tiers high. She placed her book gently on the top shelf, remembering that it was just last summer that Fen had made it for her. She had wanted the children to have real books they could look at during school; and she needed a place to put them, she had said. Nora ran her hand across the smoothly crafted wood of the shelves and smiled, remembering how Grable had teased Fen about those clay pots. He was surely no potter, Grable had said. A farmer, certainly. A skilled shepherd, undoubtedly. A fine horseman and a decent carpenter, but please, Grable had insisted, Fen's skill had reached its boundaries when it came to pottery.

She cleared her throat and turned back towards Fen,

trying so much to speak casually and to act what she thought "normal" might be, as if her best friend had not just buried his father, as if war was not looming ominously.

Fen gave Aegius a nod in the direction of the door and turned to Nora when it was shut behind him.

"Any news?" she asked.

"News about what?" he answered with a smile. The two sat down on a long wooden bench underneath one of the small square windows.

"I don't know," she sighed. "News about Oktahn or Sabian and Wylla, news about when Dresdor might invade… I don't know."

"I do have news. Sort of."

She looked up at him with very serious eyes, surprised to find that his did not seem nearly so somber.

"Good news, in fact. At least—I think so."

A mixture of relief and wonder washed over Nora as Fen fairly beamed now.

"Do you remember the first time we got caught in a southern storm together? The very first… we'd been playing at the creek by Tullian's sheep pen?"

"And you were adamant that you had to get me back to my home, and my mother gave us mugs of chocolate by the fire. Yes. We were little."

"I was eight, and your father thanked me for bringing you home safely. And I wanted to marry you then."

He said the words as if they were the most obvious natural ones he could have said, but Nora was as stunned as if he had said he had gone to the moon. She tried awfully hard to think of something clever to say, but the words would not cooperate in the least.

"And then I wanted to marry you every day after that," Fen continued, "though I did not believe your father would ever give his daughter to a man with no family or standing, no prospects…"

What was he saying? Nora's brain was flying all over the place trying to make sense of his words, and for the love of all things noble why could she not come up with one coherent thing to say? All she managed to finally get out was a "hmm", as if he had just said something utterly inconsequential like "wouldn't it be nice to have a picnic today?" and she had answered with a polite "hmm." Honestly, could she have come up with a more dreadful response?

"But now that my situation is different," Fen said as he got down on his knee, "I wonder if you would be my wife?"

She looked at him a long time before finally whispering, "I would have been your wife whatever your situation."

Fen pulled out the silver band that Westerlyn had worn and put it on her finger. "I know that. But I think going to your father as a royal heir and not a farmhand may have aided my cause."

Nora looked breathlessly from the smooth, glimmering ring to the dark brown eyes that were staring so deeply at her. "You'll want to wait till all this war mess and madness is over," Nora began, "That could be months, years possibly. I totally understand."

But Fen simply said, "I want to marry you tomorrow."

18

UNIONS

It was a quiet affair. Few men at the camp had any idea that in a small stone chapel north of the Lawksbur in the charming town of Faircross, the Commander of the Resistance was marrying the girl he had brought home safely all his life. The Elders stood before the small gathering (save Huros who was yet gone), and Xophnius led the couple through the vows of the Winderlawk marriage rite.

Mohrly Wrenvale, Nora's father, stood beside his daughter. He was not an exceptionally warm fellow, but he wore as proud a smile as Nora had ever seen on his face. Emaliys stood at his side, dressed (for the first time that Nora had ever seen) in traditional Ahlrik array with garlands of flowers woven through her auburn hair and about her gown. Aegius, Liam, and Khaz stood next to Fen, wearing their finest, with gleaming sabers at their sides.

Xophnius had hung a thick robe of navy blue trimmed in shimmering silver about Fen's shoulders and placed a gleaming platinum circlet on his head. Nora too wore a thin band around her brown locks and held a simple bunch of white peonies.

It was not the wedding most girls dream of, and most certainly not all that you would expect for a royal wedding. But it was the wedding Nora had always dreamed of, for she was standing next to Fen, and beyond that there was little for her to be bothered with.

What they lacked in fanfare they possessed in delight.

When the vows had been said, the couple kneeled solemnly. Phlycia and Bryn stood before Nora with their hands on her shoulders, while Xophnius and Kholrihk did likewise with Fen; and the Elders, with much joy, bestowed their blessings on the young man and woman.

At a different point in history there would have been feasting for weeks throughout the Four Corners of the Earth. Fen and Nora would have journeyed far together throughout the kingdom, being gladly received and happily celebrated by their people. But this was not that point in history. And that was not the hour chosen for them.

Rather, Fen and Nora returned quietly to the Lawk farm, where the three riders were just back from Valdestria. And it was not a honeymoon that began but a war council instead. The usual leadership assembled in their meeting room to hear the news that Sabian brought. But as he began to speak, Fen interrupted.

"Aegius, where is Liam?"

He shook his head, "I have not seen him since earlier. My apologies, I did not tell him to come straight back; we were not expecting the three till evening."

"We have ridden the wind as well as we might," Sabian answered. And their appearance showed the demands of their journey. Strands of Wylla's hair were blown wild and loose all about. The three were covered in dust, and the others all now noticed the blood-tinged bandage around Sabian's arm.

"Do you need attention?" Aegius looked sharply at his arm, but Sabian shook his head and proceeded to inform them of his alarming encounter with Benriys and the claims he had made. Huros shared also that several of the dissenters had gone missing and were presumed dead, Pertius among them.

"The Norians are getting rid of anyone who dare to stand against them now," Sabian glared. "And Dresdor is blind to it."

"Then we must help them see it, brother," Fen replied.

"You shall have the chance to tell them yourself in the morning," said Sabian, "for the troops are not five leagues to the northeast. We nearly came out on top of them after crossing through Steadhill and were forced to cut farther west. Their number seems..." He did not finish his sentence, and a heavy silence fell over the group with his words.

At last Fen spoke up. "Well I hope it seemed enormous. We could use an enormous army; there is an enemy to be fought. We only need to convince Dresdor that the enemy is not us."

As expected, it was not long after dawn when the blue banners of Dresdor could be seen flying in the morning sky as the ranks of Dresden soldiers filed across the low-lying hills of Ainsworth.

At the camp, the men of the Resistance stood quietly at attention, though weapons were to be strictly at rest. A tension ran through the camp like a nerve that might snap at any moment, but the men followed their orders and waited, watching the northern landscape fill with Dresden troops.

It was already unpleasantly warm even at the early hour, when Fen joined the Elders and the others outside. Nora watched Fen from the doorway of the farmhouse, trying to avoid glancing northward. Just knowing that an army was coming had been awful; the actual sight of them made her stomach turn. *Surely they will come to peace without fighting,* Nora tried to assure herself. *Surely the Elders will find a way.* And then she thought back over the Elders'

Writings and how many accounts they told of battles waged and uprisings launched, and her heart sank. The history of the tribes was full of conflict and trouble; was it really likely they would resolve their differences and come together this time?

Well, whatever may unfold, she could not go on allowing such gloomy pessimism to poison her thoughts, and she made up her mind to find her mother and see what work she would make herself busy with.

Between the Dresdens to the north and the Resistance to the south, four people were at work in the open space in the middle. Liam and Khaz were two of these, raising a large white canvas flying atop a tall wooden post. Two of the Dresdens were doing the same, for this is where the leaders of each side would conference together before any action was taken.

Khaz spoke quietly to his brother as they worked. "There are five thousand of them if there are a dozen. We are outnumbered at least four to one."

"More than that," Liam muttered back. "But we can't worry about that right now."

"Can you think of anything else we should worry about at the moment?"

Liam did not answer, and the two brothers went about finishing their work.

Fen watched with the Elders and his advisors as they waited for the meeting ground to be prepared.

"I'll not lie," Fen tried to lighten the mood, "I'm surprised to see you in mail, Xophnius... all of you." He gestured to the five Elders, who were all dressed in smart garments of the finest silver mesh. "I suppose I thought you were rather invincible."

Xophnius smiled and shook his head. "There is no wound from which we may not recover—it is true. But do not imagine that the injuries are pleasant."

"The grave ones may take rather some time to heal," added Bryn. "Isn't that right, Xophnius?"

The Elders all smiled, obviously recalling some shared experience unknown to the others.

But Xophnius replied indignantly, "I hardly think this is the time to recount such disastrous incidents."

"It was disastrous to your pride above all, friend," Bryn said, not meanly, but all the same she ceased to speak of it.

Noticing the wedding band on Fen's hand, Sabian blurted out, quite without thinking, "You've been busy while I was gone. Do you really think this was the time?"

"I think the time may always be found to do the important things," Fen answered.

At that moment they were interrupted by a stirring in the camp. There was a commotion coming from the west, and Thasperus and Tullian were briskly making their way through the ranks to where Fen stood.

"The men of Winderlawk have come, Commander," Tullian announced with an unmistakable pride.

"Five hundred from north and south," beamed Thasperus, "ready to serve under the wild youth who has been to the Caves and back."

They could be seen now, marching east across the field to the Resistance camp, and their coming did quite a lot of good actually. For though there had certainly been some Winn who had already joined the troops, they had undeniably been a small number compared to the Ahlrik and the Kysmen; and there had been resentment borne by many over this. But to see hundreds marching to join them in the hour that counts most, the men of the Resistance raised a shout of welcome.

Fen stopped Tullian as he turned to join the newcomers, "Is Oktahn among them by any chance?"

"No, Commander, I don't believe so."

"Well, they have already heard they are welcome from the men," Fen said, "Please tell them I am honored they have come." Then looking northward, he said to the others, "It appears they are ready for us. Shall we go?"

Nora watched keenly as they made their way to the white flags flapping softly in the breeze. A wooden table had been placed between them, where both sides were now coming together. On one side Fen took his seat with Aegius sitting to his right and Sabian to his left. The five Elders stood tall behind the three men, looking fully awe-inspiring, in some way that no one could quite put their finger on.

Across the table three Dresden took their seats. These were, first, the High General Lyhnge, along with one of his captains, as well as an officer who represented the Regent of Dresdor. This officer, known as Wainright, unfolded a document he carried and was preparing to read it aloud, but Fen spoke first.

"High General Lyhnge, though these circumstances are unfortunate, I am pleased to meet you all the same. I have heard you to be a man of honor and virtue."

Lyhnge bowed his head graciously, with a quick glance at Huros. "I hear the same of you, sir." Then looking from Fen to Sabian, he greeted him as well. "Lord Dresbane, I am always pleased to see you, though I bitterly wish we did not find ourselves on opposite sides of this line. There are many here who share that feeling… who are grieved to be at odds with so fine a tribesman as yourself."

"Perhaps there is time still to remedy that, sir," replied Sabian hopefully.

Wainright seemed quite antsy with the tone of the greetings and restless to get on with what he had come to do.

"You have something to read to us, friend,"

prompted Fen. "Please do. We have things to share with you as well."

Wainright stood and proceeded in a very official sounding manner to read something very like what was heard in Parliament—the call of the Regent of Dresdor to bring the tribes to their rightful place under Dresden rule for the good of the kingdom... and other such condescending and imperious sounding notions.

It went on rather longer than the others had expected, and just when Sabian thought it quite impossible to bear another word, the proclamation abruptly came to an end and Wainright resumed his seat.

Next Fen took a deep breath and began his response. "Friends, I have two main points to raise in objection to your cause. In the first place, I believe you have been led along toward this ambition under a sinister pretense. There are men among your ranks whom you certainly know to support this war, but I wonder if you know who works behind them to push you to your ruin. I will ask the Lord Dresbane to speak briefly on this."

Sabian placed on the table the ivory whistle and the linen, with the initials B.T.N. monogrammed in the corner.

"You will know the man to whom these belonged," Sabian began.

"I believe so," Lyhnge spoke, appearing to have no question.

"Would you also believe that Benriys attacked me in my own home not a week ago?" He lifted his arm slightly, calling attention to the bandaged injury. "According to him, the Norians have a long loyalty to Ahmahnric who has not shockingly been gathering his own army."

Wainright broke in here with a few stuttering starts at an objection, but Lyhnge silenced him and asked Sabian to continue.

"This conflict we are on the edge of accomplishes little besides cutting down our own numbers. After it, we will be unable to match the strength of his force. And he will have what he wants, which is control of the Four Corners. The Norians will have what they want, which is the ease and wealth of a new life. But I am afraid Dresdor—not to mention the other tribes—will be ruined if not completely destroyed when Ahmahnric comes to power."

Lyhnge seemed sincerely affected by Sabian's remarks, as did his captain who leaned over and whispered something in the general's ear. But Wainright replied rather scornfully, "You may rank above most of the tribe, Lord Dresbane, but I am fairly sure you do not rank above the Regent himself. Interesting as your story may be, he issued this resolution—"

Fen interrupted him politely, "Thank you, sir; you bring me to my second point."

You can imagine the sense of agonizing anticipation that filled the troops on both sides as they looked on quietly, unable to hear or know what was being said. It seemed a thick silence had fallen over the whole region, as if even the birds themselves knew that weighty things were unravelling and they dared not interrupt.

Fen continued. "The business of the Regent is to govern in the king's absence, is it not?"

"Of course it is," huffed Wainright.

"How should we rightly proceed then, High General, if the king's heir is no longer absent but ready to take his throne?"

At once all three Dresden looked at Sabian, who gave a sheepish look in return. "It is not me, brothers."

Lyhnge looked back very seriously to Fen, "You believe you know who the rightful king is?"

Aegius sensed their skepticism and felt his muscles

tighten, his jaw clench. He looked past the Elders to where Liam, Khaz, and Wylla stood just behind them. Liam's expression told him they were ready to act should anything unexpected erupt.

Fen looked at the general directly and answered plainly, "I am he."

It seemed none of the three sitting across the table knew exactly what to say for a moment, and at last one of the Elders finally spoke. It was Kholrihk. "Certainly you will need time to consider what has been brought before you this morning."

"It is quite a claim," Lyhnge replied. "How many have heard this?"

"Few beyond this table," said Fen.

The general questioned Huros with an intense look, to which Huros nodded with certainty.

The captain again leaned over with a whisper to his general while Wainright sat there looking completely dumbfounded. Lyhnge nodded to his comrade and then addressed Fen.

"Of course we will need to see some sort of evidence to support your claim to the throne."

An entirely reasonable response—how could Fen have overlooked that they would surely want as much? And what did he have to give them? But he heard Aegius's voice over his racing thoughts.

"I have it." Aegius looked back to his siblings and nodded to Liam, who joined them at the table. "I have the entire record of his lineage. It is at a safe place."

This news took even the Elders by surprise. Liam, too, seemed uneasy that such knowledge was being shared.

"Liam, go to the vault. Bring the Records of the Watch." Turning from Liam to the other men Aegius added, "It is a distance, but if he leaves now he can be back by morning. The scrolls plainly trace him all the way to Kembarius."

"Then let him go. And let us see these records in the morning," said Lyhnge.

Both sides dispersed and returned to their respective camps. Liam was off in minutes, headed northwest across the hills. And a wave of relief, however temporary, seemed to ripple across both sides gathered there in Ainsworth.

The relief was all the greater when later that evening, Sabian stood at the door of the farmhouse, knocking eagerly. Nora led him into the kitchen where she and Xophnius and Fen had been deep in discussion. Sabian presented a letter to Fen from the High General, which Fen read aloud to the others:

To the Commander of the Resistance
and to the noble Elders who stand with him,

It has been a day of most startling developments. We await the records concerning your title as heir, but as to the first matter- scout reports arrived this afternoon. Barbarian troops from the East are marching with a Norian force. They are headed for Ainsworth. When they arrive, sir, it is my intention for Dresdor to stand with you.

Jeravis Lyhnge
High General of Dresdor

19

AHMAHNRIC MOVES

It was true that a force of Norians and Eastern Barbarians was marching for Ainsworth—a fierce and sizable one. What was also true, and not only true but incredibly more consequential, was that Ahmahnric himself was with them. This had not been at all his intention, but that was before he had heard the news. What exactly he heard and how he heard was like this.

The Norian troops had left Nor Que Pneuris, heading south. When they reached northern Kysmarc they halted, awaiting the Barbarians from the East who would join them for the push to Ainsworth. The Norians were several days waiting, hidden away in the mountains, when a rider arrived.

The rider spoke to no one but made his way quickly through the masses of soldiers to a tent near the middle of the grounds. Upon seeing him, the two guards standing at either side of the entrance, pulled back the canvas and closed it immediately behind him.

Kaineaux and three of his leaders stood over a small table, upon which was laid out a map of Winderlawk. They ceased speaking the moment the rider entered, and he made his way directly to Kaineaux, retrieving a sealed parchment from the satchel at his side.

Holding it out to the huge man in front of him, the rider fixed his eyes on the ground before him.

"This is from him directly?" Kaineaux demanded. The rider gave a sharp nod in reply.

Kaineaux broke the red wax and unfolded the paper, reading its contents in a matter of seconds.

"My horse!" Kaineaux growled. "I leave this minute."

"I will see to it," the rider replied and left as quickly as he had come.

"You are leaving?!" said Helsgrath, the senior captain under Kaineaux.

"I trust this to no one. Do nothing till I return. I should be no more than four days."

"Four days!?" cried Helsgrath. "And if Ahmahnric hears you have gone and the march is delayed?"

"It is Ahmahnric I am going to see," Kaineaux answered. "He is in Dresdor. Wait for our return."

"*Our* return?"

Kaineaux looked almost pleased for a moment, at least as close to pleased as is possible for someone of his sort. "He will certainly come."

And he was right. For Kaineaux reached Ahmahnric's lair in the southwestern countryside of Dresdor, near Bolkahn. When Ahmahnric read the news Kaineaux had couriered from Kysmarc himself, the cold, calculating creature became fairly electrified with a vicious hunger. An eagerness, a zeal spread through him like a piece of writing paper curls and twists when lit by a match.

"So the heir is alive and well in Ainsworth... and commanding his own little army," Ahmahnric said with a twisted grin. "They do rise up from time to time. And you are sure this is reliable?"

"Our rat inside delivered this to my scout himself," said Kaineaux. "They wait for the Dresden army like sitting fools. The heir was behind the raid at Crowbane, which was a disaster for him. He has no idea what he is doing. It will be nothing to defeat him."

Ahmahnric walked across the room to where a large black sword hung in its sheath on the wall. "Even so," he snarled, "we will take no chances." Taking the weapon in his hands he unsheathed the blade and fingered its edge. "I will go myself. And I will not leave that place while he still lives."

And so it was, that when the army from the Outer Regions was ready to leave Kysmarc for the Lawk farmhouse in Ainsworth, it was Kaineaux and Ahmahnric both who rode at their head.

Back in Ainsworth, the next morning did not unfold as smoothly as Fen and the rest of them had hoped. Liam was not back with the Records of the Watch as expected. This complicated matters greatly, for both Fen and High General Lyhnge had agreed they would wait to communicate the change in course until Lyhnge had seen the records and was satisfied with their contents. Then they were to stand side by side along with the Elders and address all of the men at once, announcing both Fen's right as the heir and their unified stand against the enemy that was coming.

However, the sun climbed the blue overhead and still Liam was not back. Equally problematic, the news that Dresdor was backing down from the War Resolution to fight *alongside* the other tribes had somehow or other leaked out—or at least bits and parts of the news had, and it was not at all well received by a great many on both sides.

Confusion and complaints, rumors and defiance spread through the ranks of both companies. Some were relieved and encouraged by the news; others were furious.

"I thought Dresdor was going to rule the Four Corners?!" raged one of the Dresden lieutenants to Lyhnge. "Did you bring us down here to conquer them

187

or do their bidding?"

"You forget your place if you think you can speak to me with such arrogance," snapped Lyhnge. "You will have your orders soon enough. At that time, before that time, and after that time your obedience is all that is required."

And it was not going much better amongst the men of the Resistance.

"Join us?" Thasperus muttered to Tullian, as a small group of Winn and Ahlrik speculated over the rumors. "What do you think would make them do such a thing?"

One of the Ahlrik was quick with his opinion. "It's a trap. Bring them in and let them learn our strengths and weaknesses… and they'll hand us all over to the enemy. Just watch."

"I don't know about that," said Tullian. "I think the Commander has a better head than to give us away so easily. He must have a reason."

One of the other Ahlrik spoke up, the sarcasm obvious in his voice, "Yes, maybe they are just late in joining us. After all, your Commander couldn't convince his own tribesmen to come until yesterday."

Thasperus lunged at the man, but Tullian grabbed him tightly, holding him back.

Meanwhile Fen sensed time was running short. "What do you think?" he asked Aegius. The Elders and his advisors all sat at the round wooden table in the house, weighing the dilemma carefully.

"I think he must be back at any minute," Aegius replied earnestly.

"Perhaps he had trouble finding the scrolls?" suggested Fen.

But Aegius shook his head. "Impossible."

Then Khaz spoke. "Let me go after him. Perhaps his horse has gone lame. There is nothing between here and the vault, and if he has been forced to go on foot we will be long in waiting."

Several around the table nodded at this reasoning.

"I think it is all that can be done at the moment," said Xophnius.

"Then let me go," Sabian urged, standing to his feet.

"Certainly not," said Fen. "You have done more than your share with the ride to Valdestria, and you are injured at that."

But Sabian was emphatic. "The wound is nothing. And besides, if I am the one to go I think the High General and my tribe will be inclined to be patient."

Huros supported this assertion, and in the end it seemed likely the most promising path to take. And so, after conferring with Aegius about his route, Sabian rode off once again with speed.

The house was dark that night and still, as Fen stood at the window, looking out on the moonlit field of soldiers sleeping. He turned at the sound of a soft creaking of the plank floor. Nora stood there, in a fog between sleep and wake. He smiled at her but there was a pain in his eyes; she could see that instantly, dark as the surroundings were and dream-soaked as her vision still was.

"It is the middle of the night. What are you doing?" she asked.

He looked as if he were about to speak, as if he wanted to; but the next moment he simply turned back to the window and gazed out pensively.

"You must sleep; please come back to bed," Nora gently urged him.

"I am afraid I have sent them both into a trap."

"They will come tomorrow," she said. She walked over to his side and took his hand, placing her head on

189

his shoulder. "You'll see."

Fen shook his head gravely. "Ahmahnric has them."

Nora snapped wide awake at those words. "What in the Four Corners makes you say that?"

He did not reply anything at first; and though reluctant to press him, Nora could not resist placing her hand on the side of his face, begging ever so slightly for a response. Though he remained fixed on the window, he tried his best to give her an answer.

"How did I know I loved you, Nora? I just knew. How did I know Aegius spoke the truth down in that cellar? My whole life I have dreaded—feared—knowing the truth for some reason; and yet when he spoke, I knew it to be true... as surely as I knew I loved you..." and now at last he turned to his young wife, "...as surely as I know Ahmahnric has Liam and Sabian."

She read the grieved seriousness in his face, feeling that she might almost be swallowed up in it. "Well," she said as hopefully and confidently as she could, "you will get them back. Won't you."

Fen looked at Nora with the saddest of smiles, and she noticed how pale he seemed in the silver moonlight. He kissed her forehead and took a deep breath, "Yes, I will." He put his arms around her and pulled her close; and she could have sworn for a moment that she heard him whisper three tiny words. No, it was silent. But in years to come she would recall that night and wonder if she had not really heard them:

I am sorry.

20

EXCHANGE AT A HIGH PRICE

Liam and Sabian did not come the following day as Nora had so hoped. Nor did they come the day after that. And when someone finally did come, it was not what anyone on either side hoped for, though it was what they had all come to expect. It at least brought a close to the grim business of waiting, for the end was unmistakably rushing upon them now.

Fen and Aegius were out amongst the men, when two Kysmen scouts came flying on horseback into the camp with the news.

"They have come!"

The leaders of both sides made immediately for the middle ground between the camps, where the riders were dismounting.

"They have come!" repeated one of them, breathless and anxious. "And their number is easily more than these two forces combined."

"How far now?" Fen pressed.

"A league to the east at most."

"Well, sir," Fen looked to the Dresden general, "are we to make peace with each other... and go to war together?"

"I do not know what other choice we have under the circumstances," Lyhnge replied. "We will see if they come with terms that may be accepted. My men will be ready if they do not."

Lyhnge and the soldiers with him left. Aegius too

turned to go, saying, "I will let the captains know their men are to assume their positions."

But Fen grabbed his arm, pulling him away a few meters and speaking to him alone for several minutes. Aegius nodded soberly at last; and when Fen turned and headed straight for the house, Aegius went immediately to find Khaz and Wylla.

No one saw as Fen and Nora said goodbye in the little farmhouse. And in the heightened state of things outside, neither did anyone really notice when, not much later, Fen put Nora on her horse and sent her away in the company of Wylla and Khaz. They were soon out of sight and headed far from the darkness that was rolling in like a plague.

The sun was high and the air sweltering. The smell of horses and sweat seemed everywhere, and restlessness simmered like scalding water ready to boil.

Fen and High General Lyhnge positioned themselves at the eastern front of the troops, with Dresdor spread behind them northward and the Resistance to the south. Just behind the two commanders were Aegius, the five Elders, and three of the Dresden captains. Astride their mounts, they all stood strong as stone, ready for battle, watching the eastern horizon.

And they came. By the hundreds—by the thousands. For what seemed entirely too long, the men who had been waiting in Ainsworth watched the eastern landscape fill with the sneering faces of soldiers from the Outer Regions. The quiet of the countryside was rent with the clashing of metal as they beat their shields with their sword hilts and taunted the whole earth with the swells of their guttural war cries.

The front ranks were entirely Barbarians from the East, a people generally tall, lean, and pale as ghosts. All of them wore headdresses made from the bone and skin of various animals, and as they carried on with the shouting and beating of their shields, a chant began emerging from the chaos. As it was in their native tongue, no one from the Four Corners could begin to decipher the words, though the meaning plainly transcended language. They had come to bring doom, and they were thirsty to unleash it.

Norian troops were piled up behind the Barbarians in vast number—not quite so savage in their appearance but no less seething with hatred. They had been out-dwellers long enough, while the tribes of the Four Corners had enjoyed lands that were fruitful and abundant, free from the bitter winters of Nor Que Pneuris and the scarcity that they brought year after year. The time had come; with Ahmahnric, the Norians finally had their chance to rise up against the tribes and claim what they had so long craved.

After a long while, their battle lines began to part in the middle, beginning at the far back, as a party of six riders came single file down the path cleared for them. Like a wave, the Norians and the Barbarians hushed as the men passed by, so that by the time they finally made their way to the front, all was eerily quiet across the low-lying hills.

The six rode forward toward the men who stood ready to meet them; and as they came close Fen's heart sank, for he saw that Sabian was among them. At the head of them, a man rode a coal-black stallion larger than any beast Fen had ever seen before. Looking into the rider's eyes Fen thought he might have met a wolf had he not seen the body of a man and known that he was coming face to face with Ahmahnric.

The threatening figure who took his place next to Ahmahnric was clearly Kaineaux, and a man masked in the familiar brown leather hood rode to his side leading a horse who bore the fourth member of the party. This was Sabian, though if you did not know him somewhat well you might not have immediately recognized him.

His hands were tied at his back, and his head hung heavily forward even though he tried valiantly to hold it up. His face was cut and bruised, one eye swollen shut; and the dark stains of blood on his clothes told a brutal story. Two mounted soldiers stood guard behind these four with swords drawn.

Huros, so deeply pained at the sight of Sabian, was about to speak, but Xophnius held up his hand and stayed him.

"Ahmahnric!" Xophnius boomed. "It is no less wretched to see you now than it has always been."

"Likewise, you stupid fool," Ahmahnric replied coolly. And then he fixed his eyes of steel on Fen. "I found something you lost."

Sabian managed to lift his head just enough to see Fen's face for a moment. "I am… ever so sorry," he gasped.

Lyhnge spoke before Fen could say anything. "And you've brought him here for a reason, I assume. What do you want?"

Ahmahnric smiled. "Yes. Well, you see, I do *not* want this kinsman of yours actually. In fact, I am prepared to give him to you *at this very moment.*" The words dripped from his tongue enticingly.

"Is that so?" Huros interjected angrily. "And what devil scheme do you have in mind?"

Ahmahnric ignored Huros altogether, staring intently and only at High General Lyhnge now. "Do you know the high, high price I require for the life of this one man?"

"Just get on with it," Lyhnge barked.

"Go home," Ahmahnric replied breezily, waving his

arm freely towards the northeast. "Go back to Dresdor and take all your men. Keep your lives and go home to your families, with your wounded friend. He is alive yet... partly. That is more than generous, wouldn't you say?"

A cold feeling, hollow and bleak, settled over Fen, as he realized what was unfolding.

"Do not... please..." Sabian mumbled hoarsely.

"You coward!" bellowed Xophnius. "You shameless stench of a beast!" His mare stamped and grew agitated under her impassioned master.

"Do not speak in haste, sir," said Phlycia calmly to Lyhnge.

Lyhnge glanced ever so briefly at Fen, and the young commander saw what he feared—a conflicted man, considering the terms.

"Tomorrow," Fen answered Ahmahnric himself. "We will give you your answer in the morning." Then he looked at the High General, "Isn't that right?"

Lyhnge eventually nodded his agreement.

Ahmahnric was not at all pleased with this. His icy gaze lingered long on Fen, and then he simply turned and beckoned his men after him, in apparent acceptance of their response.

Back at the house, the council that followed long into the night was as heated and intense as you might have expected. Phlycia alone sat; the others stood or paced like wild animals in a cage desperate to spring out.

"You cannot give into his ploy. It is as simple as that." It was Kholrihk, pressing the case with Lyhnge.

"I'm afraid it is not at all as simple as that," replied Lyhnge. "And if you think it is, I fear you stand to be horribly disappointed."

Bryn's eyes flashed with anger. "If you and your men abandon the tribes, you know full well you leave them to their deaths."

"Madam," answered Lyhnge carefully, leaning imposingly across the wooden table, "perhaps you forget that we came first to defeat them ourselves."

"Indeed!" Huros nearly shouted, his voice rattling the very walls. "A purpose based upon nothing but lies from an enemy now exposed to you... whom you somehow even still prefer to ally yourself with! When did Ahmahnric become so great a friend of Dresdor?!"

"Huros," hummed Phlycia softly, "you'll not win him like this." Her voice, though calm, had an arresting quality over the whole room. In fact, it was difficult to know if the warm glow that was cast about came from the lamp that stood behind her chair or from the Ahlrik Elderess herself, who had on more than a few occasions, by her quiet secrets, wrought peace when all was at the edge of disaster.

"You must know that if you flee today, you will only be his target tomorrow," said Aegius.

"Indeed we likely will," agreed Lyhnge. "But consider that many of my men already prefer to walk away sooner than fight with you. And now in doing so, they may rescue their tribesman. Even if I gave the order to stay, I cannot even be sure it would be obeyed."

"Perhaps you underestimate the respect your men have for you," said Fen.

"No, friend," he answered almost apologetically, "you underestimate the lack of respect they have for you... and your men."

"That is a fine way to speak to the man who is to be your king!" said Xophnius. And the general meekly bowed his head and raised his hands in a gesture of surrender.

"In truth I mean no offense," said he. "For myself, though I have yet to see the proper evidence, I suspect you are very well the rightful heir else you would not have the Elders behind you. But I am of an older school than most. You must know that we are beyond the age of Elder opinion holding sway over the masses. I cannot compel my men to stand with you... especially when they will find the terms offered so agreeable."

Xophnius and Kholrihk both began spouting objections and unpleasantries, as Phlycia tried again to calm them. Huros simply left the room, letting the door slam with a hard clash behind him. And Fen noticed that Aegius had grown altogether distant and brooding.

"We will find Liam," Fen said quietly as the others argued on.

Aegius responded with a look of fearful doubt. "Sabian was useful to them alive. But Liam? They had no reason to let him live... and they needed no reason to kill him."

"We cannot know that they even found him," replied Fen, though not convincingly. "We must not assume the worst."

Aegius was not comforted. "If they did not find him, then where is he?"

And now things had reached a point of seeming hopelessly thick and muddled, so that everyone eventually fell silent, feeling there was really not much more that could be said.

Lyhnge was clearly not happy with the choice as it had been laid before him but felt his hands were very much tied. One of his captains was similarly conflicted; the other was unapologetically relieved at the way the situation was unfolding. The other tribes were going to be defeated, and the work would not even be Dresdor's. Yes, they would have to stand up to Ahmahnric at some point, but let Dresdor build their forces in the meantime. They would be ready when he came.

As for the Elders, even Phlycia wore the discouragement of the situation plainly. And it was Fen who finally said, "Let us admit there is nothing more that may be done together tonight and be finished. Certainly we all need what little time remains to come to terms with what tomorrow will demand of us. Good general, if you do not see the practicality of fighting with us, I confess I pray you will at least see the rightness of it."

Lyhnge felt a jab of shame, and though he said nothing in reply, he did bow deeply and sincerely as he left the room with the rest of the Dresden company.

The winds were blowing from the south when morning came, great smokestacks of clouds gathering in the distance. At least there would be no mastids riding in on the wings of the storm that was coming.

The men of the Resistance had stood armed and ready since dawn, steeling themselves for the test that lay before them. The men of Dresdor had not prepared themselves to join the fight, for rumor had it that they were leaving. But neither had they prepared to leave, for when it came down to it—even amongst the most zealous Dresden—somehow the actual business of turning and walking away felt unhappily like a snake slithering quietly off into the woods. And no man likes the look of himself in that light. It was a strange atmosphere about the place... and a strange way to begin the day that the Four Corners were to be won back from the brink of desolation.

Lyhnge had been embarrassingly late emerging from his tent, the sign of a man who could not come to a conviction he could live with. But when he finally did show himself, he and his men silently mounted their horses, joining Fen and company in the sober ride to the front lines.

The winds held low as Ahmahnric and his party rode forward under the troubled, gray skies. Sabian was very nearly slumped over the neck of his horse and not conscious in any meaningful way.

The Elders were all watching the High General, for it was assumed he would be the one to give the verdict. They were surprised then, as was everyone, when it was Fen who spoke. And he did not speak first to Ahmahnric or the High General or to anyone gathered right there. But he raised his voice and filled the hillscape with it.

"Men of the Four Corners!" He wheeled his horse around to address both armies gathered behind him, who were watching with their whole bodies and listening with their souls. "We sold our brotherhood long ago... for far too cheap a price. I aim to buy it back today! The traitor has something that belongs to us!"

He glanced back to Ahmahnric with nothing but defiance in his eyes. "I would like the Dresbane back!" It was breathlessly quiet across the grassy hills. Kaineaux sat with exceeding uneasiness on his horse, but Ahmahnric seemed quite unbothered, in fact rather enjoying the impromptu speech.

"Would you submit, brothers, to the will of one such as this?" Fen stretched out his arm and pointed to his enemy. "Would you? One who would grow his power on the backs of Slaves? On the back of your tribesman?"

Kaineaux shifted in his seat as if about to advance on Fen, but Ahmahnric stayed him for the moment.

"And yet, he has our kinsman. This I cannot accept." Fen turned abruptly, addressing his demand to Ahmahnric directly, "So I say again: I want the Dresbane back, traitor."

For a moment Fen paused and simply looked straight at Aegius with something of gratitude and apology mingled together. Then he turned back to Ahmahnric, and the words rang out, "Me for him!"

"No! NO!!" Aegius and Xophnius both shouted, Xophnius's voice bringing the weight of centuries down on the moment. But Ahmahnric's cold, smooth reply came immediately.

"Done."

The ground shifted that day, and who can say what exactly broke loose? There were so many things that began to happen all at once. The five Elders pushed and pressed for Fen to retract his words. Aegius grabbed him by the arm, pleading furiously.

"This is madness!" he said angrily. Of course he was not as angry at Fen as he was fearful, and fear is so often apt to pretend anger.

"No, brother," said Fen. "A man does not become a king by shrinking from what a good king should do."

But Aegius only clasped his arm more tightly. "No! You'll not be king; you'll be dead within the hour! Who will they follow then?"

"Who will they follow otherwise?" And then turning to Lyhnge, Fen said only one thing. "Do not waste this, sir."

It is not often that a commander of troops seasoned in war finds the words difficult in coming. But it was so for Jeravis Lyhnge on this morning. It stung in his throat as he looked humbly at Fen. "No, Your Majesty. I'll not waste it."

Within the spirits of the soldiers of all four tribes, a collective cry began to rise. It was the waking of something ancient. And not merely something historic, it was a cry of outrage. And still even more than that. For it was not outrage only, but it was an anthem of loyalty. And it swelled inside each man's heart like a squalling sea, even as the winds picked up around them with the grasses swirling wildly at their feet.

Fen broke away from his comrades and rode the few steps across to Sabian, taking the reins from his masked guide and holding them out to Huros. As Huros led his kinsman away, Fen turned once again to Ahmahnric.

"I'd like the slave too."

The hooded figure turned his head sharply, then shook it adamantly at Ahmahnric.

Both Ahmahnric and Kaineaux seemed to find this amusing for some reason.

"What makes you think this slave wants anything to do with you?" asked Kaineaux.

"I believe he was one of my men… who lost his way." Fen looked to the man in question. "You do not have to do their foul work for them, friend."

"Perhaps our 'foul work' is not as unpleasant to him as you think," replied Ahmahnric. "Let us test it." He turned to the man in the brown leather hood and said as calmly as any words in the human tongue might be said, "Kill him."

The man unsheathed his sword, and Aegius started immediately to Fen's side, but Fen refused him to come. "I am not rightly yours to watch now, Aegius."

The sword visibly shook in his hand, as the rider seemed ponderously reluctant to strike Fen with it. A peal of thunder rolled heavily across the skies which were growing ever darker.

"Or perhaps he is right," said Kaineaux with disdain. "Have you had a change of heart… *slave*?" Then with disgust, Kaineaux reached over and jerked the leather hood from the man's head. But it was not Oktahn's blue eyes and scarred face they found unmasked.

It was Liam.

21

BATTLE FOR THE FOUR CORNERS

"Liam!!" Aegius yelled with a howling rage.

The winds were beginning to whip as the rains let loose now.

"He did not deserve it!" Liam shouted as tears fell, tears of shame and grief and years long with bitterness. "Father did not deserve to die. And *he* does not deserve to be king!"

"Liam, no!" pleaded Fen, "This is not the way."

"It is insanity!" Aegius barked.

Ahmahnric watched quietly for the moment with a glimmering light in his pale eyes. He found the scene as it was unfolding immensely satisfying.

A coarse, biting laugh choked its way from Liam's throat. "Is it, Aegius?! We have spent our years watching over this weakling who would undo it all of his own choosing in this very moment. Yes, perhaps you are right," his voice grew angrier, "it does sound very much like insanity!"

The shock and grief wrestled wildly in Aegius's voice, "Think of father, Liam!"

"I didn't know my father!" he bawled in return.

Ahmahnric's command was stone cold. "Do it."

Liam let out a loud cry as he raised his sword, but he did not strike. For Xophnius had reached for the knife at his thigh and hit his mark with terrible precision. Liam crumbled forward, dropping his sword. It was a gut-wrenching sight and the beginning of a chaotic spiral. For even as Liam's friends—to say nothing of his brother—were frozen for the moment helplessly bewildered, shouts were stirring from the south.

A thunderous pounding of hooves and war cries swelled as an army of slaves came charging into view. With weapons raised, they appeared to be storming straight for an attack on Ahmahnric's army. It was very much as if they themselves were a swarm of angry mastids sent by the southern storm—with Oktahn leading the assault.

Sensing that things might very possibly swing out of his grip and quickly, Ahmahnric focused on the only thing that mattered: the young Commander who sat before him with that same self-righteous air that he had loathed in Kembarius. How many centuries now since Kembarius was planted in the ground and yet the hatred Ahmahnric had for him felt as fresh as the rain and hot as the sun. And here at last he could finish what he began ages ago. He drew his sword in one breath, and his horse leaped in the next. Before anyone knew anything, Ahmahnric had run his cold dark blade cleanly through the body of Fen Lawk.

And the Battle for the Four Corners was begun.

The soldiers of Dresdor rushed side by side with the men of the Resistance. They were joined by the newly come force from the South, and together they unleashed a holy fury upon the army of Norians and Barbarians. The battle was at once in full thrust.

Ahmahnric had given Kaineaux orders of some sort, and both had turned back to command their troops. But Kholrihk was after Ahmahnric like lightening, and the two disappeared in the fray of battle. Bryn marked Kaineaux, and these two were soon engaged fiercely, weapons flying. If size and strength alone won battles, he would have overpowered her in a blink. But he lacked both her speed and skill and was enraged to find himself struggling to match her.

Aegius, Xophnius, and Phlycia were on the ground next to Fen almost at once. They worked like madmen possessed to wrap his chest and stop the blood that was leaking out all too quickly.

"There is breath," said Phlycia as she leaned over him closely. "It is so slight, but it is there."

The chaos of combat was all around them, but Lyhnge himself stood guard as if he were six men.

"Quickly!" said Xophnius, taking Aegius's hands and placing them over the red-soaked wound. The rain was pouring in buckets as he tore a long swath of cloth from his own outer garment and carefully ran it under Fen's body, wrapping it over again and tying it as tightly as he dared.

"There, friend. Be easy," he spoke like a father to Fen but the trembling nervousness in his voice was impossible to miss. Then he looked at Aegius, "We must get him inside—help me."

Their horses had been scattered with the onrush of soldiers, and they were just preparing to carry him, when they heard a shout.

"Xophnius!" It was Oktahn, guiding his horse towards them through the mayhem. "What can I do!?" he shouted as he reached them and saw that it was as awful as he feared.

"Take him to the house!" Xophnius directed, and they positioned Fen as best they could in front of Oktahn, who dug his heels into the horse's flesh and made all speed to the farmhouse.

"There are things at my camp I must bring," Xophnius said quickly as the three forced their way through the fighting and rain towards the house. "Can you manage him till I am back, Phlycia?"

She hesitated anxiously for just a breath, blinking back rain drops and looking helplessly unsure, but Aegius answered before she could speak anyway, quite emphatic, "No! You cannot leave him. Let me go. What do I need?"

Outside the battle raged on until late in the afternoon. The men of the Four Corners fought together as brothers, as had not happened in the history of the tribes since the reign of Kembarius. They might have perhaps overpowered Ahmahnric's forces on their own by sheer fury. But then there was also the army from the South that Oktahn had mustered, making victory almost certain.

They pushed Ahmahnric's men back farther and farther east, as the rains continued to pour and drench the battle grounds. There is much to tell that you would likely want to hear... how Thasperus and his troop of northern Winn won medals of valor for their stand at the Lawksbur when an enemy brigade attempted to flee north. How High General Lyhnge thwarted a Norian attack on the house where Fen lie under Xophnius's care. How Kaineaux died, in the end, at his own doing, and how heroes were made on that day who would be sung about for ages.

Indeed, if you were to read the later Writings of the Elders, you would learn much of the heroics in the Battle for the Four Corners. But certainly at present we must return to the small farmhouse, where Fen had been taken by faithful Oktahn and cared for painstakingly by Xophnius and Phlycia.

He lay motionless on the same bed in which Grable had lain not so very long ago. Xophnius stood over him, with a small needle and silverish thread-like line, stitching now after doing what he could for the deeper wounds the blade had inflicted. Ahmahnric's sword, being nyloth, had pierced through Fen's mail cleanly, and there was no denying that his condition was dire.

"Will he come through?" asked Aegius, who was pacing the room after returning from Xophnius's camp.

The Elder made no response but only kept meticulously to the work at hand. Phlycia stood across from Xophnius with a lantern casting its pale, clear light over Fen's chest. She looked up at Aegius sympathetically.

"The tonic you have brought will clean the wounds," she said gently. "And this serum is a powerful healing agent. It is all that can be done."

"Yes, but do you think he will come through it?" Aegius pressed.

Now Phlycia was the one who did not respond. She looked away quickly, wiping away something that seemed to be in her eyes and quietly focused once again on Fen.

She and Xophnius mumbled back and forth occasionally to each other, too low for Aegius to understand what they were saying. He felt as if the whole world was unravelling, and truly, for Aegius, was it not? The reality of his own brother's treachery haunted his thoughts mercilessly, yet he grieved his death all the same. Everyone knows that it is a dreadful thing to grieve a person's death, but it is cruel twist to grieve their death and their life with the same tears.

Hours passed. The rains ceased. The fighting had shifted far to the east now so that a quiet was given back to the farm, though certainly it is a mournful quiet that follows battle. The five Elders were now all gathered with Aegius in the room where the heir lie perilously close to the shadow of death. Kholrihk himself was in a ghastly state from his encounter with Ahmahnric. But while he had the powers of consciousness still, he would not agree to leave Fen's room to be tended nor would he lie down to rest.

Xophnius found he could not sit for five minutes together but was relentlessly finding something—anything—to see to for Fen.

"Certainly we must keep you warm, friend," he would say and go find another blanket that he would lay carefully over his patient.

And a few minutes later, "How long has it been now... Phlycia, bring me that flask."

This went on for some time until the light outside the westward windows grew colorful with the unmistakable beauty of dusk after rain. It spilled into the room with shafts of rose and lavender hues.

Xophnius had risen to his feet once again, and this time Phlycia rose next to him and placed a hand kindly on the shoulder of her haggard friend. "He does not suffer from lack of care, but you know he is going, dear one."

Xophnius trembled and huffed and did not look Phlycia in the eyes, but only said with all the confidence he could muster, "I know nothing of the sort."

But the woman, whose tears fell freely, replied in all gentleness, "You know his wounds as well as I do. He is going, and it cannot be stopped... though you have done everything in the world that one could."

"I find that..." he stammered weakly, "I find that... very unacceptable. Very, very unacceptable."

Aegius heard her words, and it was as if her soft voice mysteriously shattered what little remained of his strength. And he wept in deep, heaving sobs.

So crushing and absorbing was the grief in the room that no one heard the bumbling sounds coming down the hall. It was not until the man was standing quite in the doorway that anyone even noticed he was there.

"Sabian," Bryn said; she was the first to see his injured form leaning against the doorframe. "No doubt you should go back and lie down, sir. You are too weak."

207

Huros agreed with her, putting Sabian's arm around his own shoulders to hold him up.

"No, please," he begged feebly. "I need to speak to the King."

"He is not able," Huros replied sadly.

And then the weakest whisper of a voice proved him wrong, "Xophnius."

They were all round the very edge of the bed in an instant, with Xophnius answering, "Yes, Fen, I am here."

His eyelids felt weighted down as with lead, but Fen struggled to open them. "Ahmahn... Ahmahnric..."

"It will be some time before Ahmahnric brings trouble to the Four Corners again," said Kholrihk.

"You've done so well today, friend," said Xophnius with a shake of emotion in his voice that he could not steady for the life of him. "*So well.*"

"And the war?" Fen mumbled breathlessly.

"It is all but won," Xophnius answered reassuringly. "You would not believe how they stood together, my boy."

Sabian, weakly fighting back his own tears, tried a few times to speak before he could manage the words, "I was not... I was not worthy of you, Your Majesty." And he slid to his knees, bowing his head against the bed.

Fen tried to lift his hand to touch Xophnius's arm but found there simply was no strength for such a feat. "You will make him," he paused to breathe heavily, "Regent... of the kingdom... yes, Xophnius?"

Sabian silently shook his head, unwillingly sending a few drops of grief splattering onto the hard plank floor. And Xophnius only said, "Let us not worry about such things right now."

But Fen drew all his might and moved his hand to touch Xophnius. He could not make his fingers grasp, but Xophnius sensed his urgency.

"Yes, yes, son," said Xophnius. "He will watch over things until…" his own voice faltered and without realizing it he braced himself against the old wooden bedpost just beside him. He closed his eyes till he had composed himself. "Truly a kingdom is built upon the kind of greatness you showed today. Of course he will watch over it as long as he must. Rest now."

Fen was growing even weaker and was so pale that his color was close to the very sheets upon which he lay. But he whispered, "I need… Aegius… please."

Aegius wanted to say how very, very sorry he was that his brother should have betrayed him… that he was so unspeakably sorry that he had not defended him when he needed him most. He wanted to cry rivers or else shout with a rage powerful enough to push back death or turn back time.

"Thank you, brother," said Fen with much effort.

"Do not thank me," Aegius replied, shaking his head and blinking away burning tears. "I… I failed you." His voice broke, and he hung his head miserably.

"No, friend," Fen pleaded faintly, "you must… never … believe that." Then he took what breath he could, and summoning the last bit of his strength he locked eyes with Aegius and said, "*Watch her.*"

And no more did Fen Lawk say.

22

THAT I SHARE FOR YOUR HOPE

News about what happened that fateful day in the little Winderlawk town of Ainsworth spread to the ends of the Four Corners and beyond. From the mountains of Kysmarc to the woods of Ahlred and the towns and cities of Dresdor, the story of Fen Lawk was told tirelessly, passionately. People from every tribe flocked to Ainsworth to pay tribute to his memory. It was not uncommon to find droves of people spending their afternoon simply sprawled out on blankets around the lawn outside the Lawk farmhouse. There was nothing particularly grand to see, just the kind of simple things that tell quiet stories of life: a small house built by hand, an old barn with a hayloft still full of straw, a bench watching the eastern horizon… a tree, strong and soaring, just near it.

Leaders from all four tribes gathered together at Cloudhaven and drafted a Declaration of Brotherhood— a treaty of peace and sworn loyalty. Sabian Dresbane was charged as Regent of the Four Corners, a post which he held faithfully for many years. But he accepted it on condition that he would not rule as a Dresbane. He was, as he insisted, Lawk's man, which is why you will never find a Dresbane regency in the history records. It was Sabian Lawksman who presided justly over the kingdom in the years following the Battle for the Four Corners and the defeat of Ahmahnric.

Of course Ahmahnric was not defeated for good and

for always; but his army was severely thrashed, and his slave holdings in the Southern Deserts were—as was seen on the day of the great battle—hugely upturned. It was years before Ahmahnric would begin again to cast his shadow over the kingdom.

Oktahn became a military commander, under Jeravis Lyhnge in fact, and led many bold raids in the Eastern Realms that were responsible for liberating hundreds, if not thousands of Slaves from the mines and the slave markets. It was two years to the day, following the great battle, that his own parents marched freely out of the mines, amazed to learn that the mysterious hero of the Slaves who had been causing such trouble for the Barbarians was their very own boy.

Neither Aegius nor Wylla nor Khaz were seen very much after the death of the heir. Aegius had travelled with the Records of the Watch to the drafting of the Declaration at Cloudhaven, but beyond that it was the rare person who sighted those who remained of the Fotterhil siblings.

Nora, likewise, virtually disappeared for quite some time. It was rumored in some parts that she was traveling alone in her grief. Others heard that she was staying with her mother's family deep in the quiet of Ahlred.

As for the Elders, Kholrihk was a very long time recovering from his injuries, with Bryn looking after him. Huros was kept busy as counselor to the Regent, and Phlycia returned to Cloudhaven and lived simply among her tribesmen.

But Xophnius. Ah! Poor Xophnius. The death of Fen weighed on him most ferociously, so that even at Cloudhaven for something as momentous as a treaty of peace and brotherhood he could find no joy, no light to his darkness. He had installed Sabian as Regent, as he had promised Fen that he would, and then he had slipped back to his cabin on the Lawksbur. For weeks upon weeks upon weeks he stayed there alone, hidden away from all society and all the outside world, until the day came when he could not and would not bear it any longer.

He opened the door and charged out into the hazy mist of the swamp. Walking straight into the thick, as if on a mission, he shouted to the treetops that obscured the sky above.

"It is impossible! You have asked the impossible!"

His feet were splashing and slogging through muck as he resolutely continued his march to the middle of nowhere.

"I have failed, Elethas! I have failed—it cannot be done! Tell me how it can be done now!!"

He halted, surrounded by enormous trees rising silently out of the dark waters all around him. He lifted his hands to the sky, and looking up, shouted with a thunderous plea, "Just take me, Elethas! Where are your horsemen!? Will they not come for me?! *Will they not come for me!!*"

His cries were met by nothing save a heavy silence and a rising mist, and yet he stood there for some time, arms uplifted. He stood there while the words of an ancient prayer of burial passed noiselessly from his lips... as though he might will Elethas to let him end his long years at that very moment. He stood there while those centuries of toil rolled through his mind and collided with the much fresher memories of a young man lying wounded in his cabin, a frightened girl with long brown hair at his side. He stood there until the quiet around him gave way to the droning of crickets and the evening air grew vibrant with the croaking songs of frogs and the wild cries of night fowl.

At last he lowered his arms to his side, utterly lost

and forlorn. His silver hair hung ragged on his shoulders, and he lowered his eyes with a pained sigh and simply began trudging back to the warm pinprick of light that just barely shone through the haze from the open door of his house.

Once inside, he did not even bother with his muckish clothes but collapsed in a chair by the fire where he sat oblivious to everything for a very long time. When at last he resigned himself to making a bit of coffee and putting on something clean, he rose to his feet and saw it.

There was a letter with his initial on the front, laying on the mantle above the hearth. *When in the Four Corners had it got there?* he wondered. He unfolded it and found his hands trembling as he read the contents:

Faithful X,

I can imagine the heartache of your bitter disappointment, as I'm sure you may try to imagine the depths of my own. Indeed, I believe that in all the Four Corners of the Earth, no one may come as near to comprehending the ocean of my sorrow as you, dear friend. Let us mourn him together, at least in heart, for we knew his greatness in our bones and we know still what his rule would have meant for the kingdom. But there is one thing that you do not know yet, that I share for your hope... as much as I may risk to disclose in such a message. You may not expect to see the Horsemen of Elethas, Xophnius. For Kembarius has an heir still, though he has not yet breathed the air of this world. And though he must carry the sore loss of never knowing his remarkable father, his father's strength is in him- I feel it even now. I am with the Watch. I dare not say where. I trust you to find us when the time is right... and that you will fulfill your ancient and future calling. Till then, friend.

N.W.L.

THE END

is yet to come.
Visit www.sarahstehlik.com for updates on future

Tales from Winderlawk